LOVE YOUR FRENEMIES

CHIC MANILA #4

MINA V. ESGUERRA

BRIGHT GIRL BOOKS

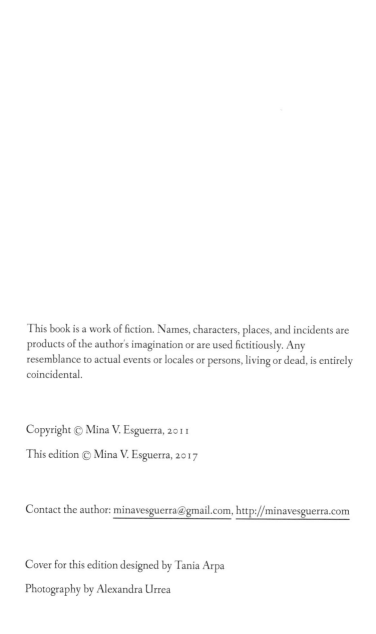

This book is a work of fiction. Names, characters, places, and incidents are products of the author's imagination or are used fictitiously. Any resemblance to actual events or locales or persons, living or dead, is entirely coincidental.

Contact the author: minavesguerra@gmail.com, http://minavesguerra.com

Cover for this edition designed by Tania Arpa

Photography by Alexandra Urrea

For my Evil Stepsisters

ONE

Tuesday
Dress fitting
Hair and makeup trial
Despedida de Soltera at Tita Chat's

THE MESSAGE from my best friend Chesca was simple and direct: *You better be here by Tuesday lunch OR I WILL KILL YOU.*

I got that not from the original email, but through the chain of people she had copied, in case I insisted on ignoring her. Still, it was Tuesday morning, and I was indeed back in Manila.

My mother did not know I was arriving that day. For months now I had only been communicating with her through courtesy texts informing her which country or city I was in. She tried to call, but I only talked to her once, and just to tell her that roaming was expensive and she should just email me if she needed to speak to me.

That was mean of me, because I thought she would

never figure out how to email. She did, but I still didn't reply.

The airport taxi dropped me off and I managed to make it to the stairs before she saw me.

"Kimberly! I swear you are going to give me a heart attack." She put down her cigarette and gave me a hug.

Like many females I can name, I had a complicated relationship with my mother. It was better now that I was twenty-seven years old, and only because we both accepted some truths about each other: That I was no longer as immature as she thought me to be, and she was not as mature as I wanted her to be.

"You didn't know I was arriving today?" I asked cautiously. Sure, she acted surprised that I was there, but Mrs. Erica Domingo was known for being dramatic every now and then.

She pressed a kiss on my cheek. "Honey, I know you're supposed to be here today, but I said I wouldn't believe it until I saw you in my house. How are you? Are you back for good this time?"

"Yes, my savings has been officially drained," I said. "I'm back home now." For better or worse.

PEOPLE HATED ME. I don't feel bad about it anymore. Everything is so relative.

Depending on the day and person you asked, I was *rude* or *manipulative* or *heartless* and other more colorful words. To the point that, when my fiancé told me that he was in love with someone else—nine days before our wedding—a bunch of people actually thought, great, Kimberly Domingo was *finally* getting punished.

How could that even happen, right? How could you get that close to a wedding and see it fall apart?

Like with most disasters, once you stepped back and really thought about it, you'd realize that it wasn't caused by just one thing.

First, there was the whirlwind romance. The time frame from first date to wedding date was a year, a short engagement.

Second, the groom-to-be had just gotten out of a relationship of several years, and though he was a great guy there were many things he hadn't worked out yet, things that came to a head embarrassingly close to our big day.

Third and maybe the most telling, the bride-to-be was me, and I was a bit of a mess.

———

THOSE WHO WANTED to see Kimberly Domingo get hers had a lot of good stuff to choose from in the weeks and months that followed my non-wedding.

It started when I found out—through a phone call in the early afternoon, to my personal phone, which I had taken while sitting at my workstation. It wasn't an office with a door, and my cubicle walls looked and felt like plastic reinforced by a layer of thin carpet. Yeah, no soundproofing when I started raising my voice.

"You're kidding me, right?" I tried to whisper, but as my former fiancé firmly explained to me that the wedding wouldn't be happening, my voice started to get loud and shrill. *"What about the caterer?"*

"We won't get our deposit back, but at least we haven't paid them in full yet."

"But my lola's already on her way!" Eighty-five years old and as we were speaking, flying in from California.

"I'm really sorry, Kimmy. But we really can't do this."

"You know what we can do? We can just shut up for a second and think about this. What happened?"

He was calm as he explained to me what his decision was, and what needed to be done. He had an answer for everything I threw at him: he was prepared to call all the companies we had booked to announce the cancellation, as well as all the guests, and was even offering to pay for a few things that I had advanced from my own account. And that I would have the money by Monday.

"Shit, Zack, I don't fucking care about the money right now! What the hell happened?"

I can't remember exactly what he said. I was in a rage, and when the phone call ended I was suddenly aware that I was in my place of work, and everyone probably heard that.

I don't remember the rest of that day. My mother told me that I came home late, but by then she already knew, because Zack had contacted her with his apologies. I have a vague memory of not wanting to go to work the next day. I remember crying into her lap, wiping tears onto the floral-patterned fabric of her nightgown, first with loud, angry sobs, and then hiccuping like a child. I had never felt like that before, ever.

Humiliated. That was the word.

IT WAS hard to go to work after that. No one said anything to my face, of course, but come on. This was an office, just like any other within the tall buildings along Ayala Avenue. It was full of people who liked to talk about other people, and in my case, with some schadenfreude. I worked at a large consumer goods company, and as an upstart management trainee was under more pressure—and given more visibility—than the average employee. Even just the rumor of wedding troubles would have been enough to earn me the top spot in all office gossip conversations, but with the scene I caused, screaming at my cellphone? I guaranteed it.

My mother told me it would get better, and eventually the office started gossiping about someone else. But I lost something, and every time I worked with someone I wondered if they respected me less. Some people at least had the benefit of hitting rock bottom in private.

The last straw was when I showed up at a meeting, months after the incident, to discover that the brief I had prepared for all participants lacked one sheet of paper. I had forgotten to print it out.

My boss at the time, not exactly the nicest person either, made a big deal out of it for fifteen minutes. While he ranted to the eight executives sitting around that conference table—also to the two regional officers on conference call with us in Shanghai and Sydney—I sat back and took it, my nails digging into the leather upholstery of my swivel chair.

"I think it's because you didn't take a break, Kimberly," he said. "I've let your mistakes the past few months slide, but this is such an amateur mistake. You've been letting your personal life get in the way of your work."

I don't need this. My side of the story? The project we were presenting was crap, and I had unwittingly given my boss a way to blame me for everything. That missing page wasn't that big of a mistake, but parading it around in front of everyone—and making it seem like I was an emotional wreck—was undoing all the years of hard work I put in.

I excused myself from the meeting, headed to HR, and

told them I was quitting. As soon as I could, I found a flight to LA.

Some people think I didn't do the right thing then, that leaving was cowardly. *I* thought so too. I had been dreading this trip back, but I knew I'd have to deal with it eventually.

TWO

What I hadn't told my mother yet was that though I was back "for good," I was planning to move out of the home I had shared with her all my life.

Estranged from my dad and sister, I lived with her in a large house in a gated community in south Metro Manila. The house was too big for us when we were a complete family; in the years since the separation it became, as far as I was concerned, a two-bedroom townhouse with three large storage rooms. And yet, not much about our routine changed: the same kind of breakfast was served every morning, the same dinner plates showed up when we had company over, my laundry basket disappeared at the same time every few days and my clothes showed up neatly pressed and folded the same way.

It became clear to me then that so much of what I knew of my life at home was determined by my mother, and she tried to make me feel like nothing had changed. I appreciated that.

What did change was that we never really saw my dad's side of the family again. But it wasn't like I hung out with my mom's family anyway—I only saw them during awkward, official gatherings like weddings and funerals, and it was that way since I was sixteen years old. My mom was a complicated woman who burned a lot of bridges; the only people who could stand her were her best friends from high school. These women, and their families, became the only family I really knew.

So it wasn't such a big deal, that thing I did. I quit my job, went to the US, and wasn't seen for a year. My mom was first to master the art of disappearing on family. What I did was tame, and shocked only the casual observers.

TAKING off was harder than I thought it would be. Not the concept of it, but the execution.

When I was younger I heard stories of teenagers who would run away. In my high school, I think a girl tried to do it. While it sounded easy in theory, I wasn't sure what she was trying to accomplish. How exactly was she going to get money? How many bags of clothes could she bring? Where was she going to stay, and how long could she stay there before someone tipped off her parents and sent her back? And, what bothered me most—what if her parents didn't want her back?

On this topic Mom was the surprisingly reliable source of information. She didn't blink when I told her that I managed to get an MNL-LAX-MNL out of what would have been two honeymoon tickets to Seoul. When I complained about not being able to pack light, she peered at my luggage critically. It was large enough to fit a human being.

"How long will you be away?" she asked.

I shrugged. "My return trip's in six months."

"You won't be spending Christmas here?"

I didn't think of that. "I guess not."

Christmas wasn't *that* big of a deal for my mother, I quickly told myself. I could remember a few Christmases in my teens when she wasn't around, either because she was on a cruise with my dad (in happier times) or with friends.

She didn't make a big deal out of it. Instead, she started picking things out of my bag. It formed a small pile on the corner of my bed. No heavy winter clothes. Just a few pairs of pants, a simple skirt, a nice dress, tops in various earth colors, a sweater, some night shirts and underwear.

"That's all you need," she said when she was done. "Anything else, you buy when you need it, or borrow. Do you have enough money?"

"I think I have enough." Despite losing money on the wedding, I had enough saved up to live on, very simply, for a while.

"It's never going to be enough. Call these people and stay with them if you're going to be around." She wrote names and numbers on a piece of paper—her trusted cousin in San Francisco, a close friend in Illinois, a former business partner in Florida. "You know what to do when you run out."

What went unsaid there was *"Ask your dad"* who was still our silent benefactor for when things went to shit. I never asked him for anything, but I suspected that he bailed us out a few times over the years.

At LAX they decided to indeed give me six months in the US, and indeed the money was never enough. But at least there was novelty, and being in unfamiliar places, encountering strange and different things every day, was a healthy distraction for the most part.

On this "sabbatical" I learned something too. I learned why my mom liked to take off. It cleared the mind, so it focused only on what mattered. I discovered what just might keep me sane when I made my way back to Manila, and the first step was to move out of my mother's house.

SO NOW THAT I was finally home, what kind of reaction did I think she would have? I wasn't just away for six months, as we had originally talked about. Instead of going back to Manila, I arranged to stay in Hong Kong instead, hopping around a few more countries in southeast Asia (visas not required), and then settling with a friend in Singapore for what would have been the longest stretch right before I came home.

"Put your dirty clothes in your laundry basket. It's still in your room," she said, no big deal, like I had come from a weekend trip.

I heard a car drive up to the house, and familiar footsteps going up the steps to our front door. I shot a panicked look at her.

She shrugged at me. "Don't look at me, dear, I'm just as surprised as you are." A moment later and she made a stealthy exit, up the stairs to her bedroom.

I contemplated running up to join her, but he was already in the house.

I didn't even hear the door, and in the next moment he was standing there in the middle of the living room. He looked different somehow—dark hair a little longer, skin suntanned instead of the run-of-the-mill *mestizo*, shoulders broader than I remembered. My heart did a little leap; the old physical responses to his presence were still there. Hated that.

"You're home," Manolo said.

It was a dance that I still knew the steps to.

He would walk into my space. His right hand would reach for my left forearm, lightly touching the inside of my elbow. His left hand would go up to the curve of my neck, thumb gently on my throat. His right arm would pull, the fingers of his left hand would nudge, and my hands would go up to cradle his jaw, leading his mouth to mine.

The first time, I sort of just ungracefully fell into the kiss, as I guess most fifteen-year-olds would. Over the years our personalities changed, we got more practice, and then I not so much *fell* as *took* a kiss from his mouth as if I was collecting what was mine. I knew he felt the same way.

THREE

Then

MANOLO MELLA. Tall, handsome Manolo Mella, son of my mom's best friend. He was three years older than me. Because our mothers were friends, he had been a fixture in my life for as long as I could remember. Even as a young guy he was cute, his features a curious cocktail of Ilocano, Ilonggo, British grandmother on his father's side, Lebanese grandmother on his mother's side. He was a model when he was barely in his teens, and he always acted too cool for us kids. He hung out at the Country Club too, but never said anything to me, Tita Chat's daughter Chesca, and Tita Rory's daughter Isabel. He spoke to me for the first time when I was a teenager.

I was fifteen, and to me he was Tita Mariela's son who was back from a year in the UK, a "gap year" he took after high school in Manila. That something I found so annoyingly *rich*, despite my family being well-off back then. He was in town to start college, and I was pretty sure our moms conspired to have us "get to know each other" because I was ordered to take her place at someone's wedding and he was the only other person there I knew.

"Oh look, it's Prince Manolo," I said, with a bad British accent. "Had enough of London? Are you here to go back to your modeling career or something?"

That was meant to be snippy. For the most part, Chesca and I rolled our eyes at each other when we heard the latest about his life. The modeling thing was actually something his mom put him up to as a child, so it wasn't like he had anything to do with it. But that was me, especially back then —snippy.

Manolo was the definition of dapper in that barong he wore to the wedding, but I tried not to let it get to me.

"Which evil stepsister are you?" he retorted.

I played with the bread knife on the table, jokingly threatening him with it. "Chesca and I look nothing alike, loser."

"I'm kidding, I know who you are," Manolo said, recovering smoothly. "You're the one who's my type."

He had that look on his face when he said that too, like he had me, which was annoying. "What's my name?"

"Kimberly Domingo."

I nodded, as if he had passed a test. "Just call me Kimmy."

We had fun that day. Chesca, Isabel and I went to this Catholic school for girls and I admittedly hadn't had much practice talking to a guy who wasn't, I don't know, *intimidated* by me. For one thing, I grew to a height that towered over a lot of guys. And those who bothered to get to know me were very polite and stuff. While Manolo was pretty much a gentleman, I noticed that he wasn't even trying to impress me. It was like it didn't matter what I thought of him.

Of course I found that intriguing.

He talked the waiter into leaving the bottle of champagne with us, and we took it out onto the hotel's pool area and finished it off ourselves. It wasn't super private; the posh hotel was in the middle of the business district, kids of different nationalities were playing in the pool, several women in bikinis were nursing cocktails while stretched out on lounge chairs.

I asked—and ridiculed him—about taking a year off after high school.

"I can't believe your parents let you do that," I said. "How do you even ask for it? 'Mom, Dad, I don't want to go to school yet. But give me money anyway, I want to experience a year of sex, drugs, and rock and roll first.'"

"It's called *seeing the world*," Manolo said, not exactly in his defense. "You'll understand that when you're older."

"Fuck you. You're just three years older than me." Yes, I had a foul mouth back then too.

"Why, how much would you spend on clothes and shoes for a year?" he said, and it sounded like a challenge. "Or a new bag? That's a lot of money going nowhere too."

I gasped noisily, a little offended and not hiding it. "Clothes and shoes and bags are *useful*. I use them. They're not sex, drugs, and rock and roll."

He laughed at that. "Whatever then. But I didn't take drugs."

"Then you're not so hard core after all."

He kissed me for the first time right there by the pool. By midnight we were making out, and I continued to see him that summer because it felt like a wonderful secret fling that would have angered my mother. Of course years later I realized that she wanted that all along. I wouldn't put it past her.

Well, it didn't work, at least not then. As soon as he started college, he stopped calling me, and I eventually found out from my very disappointed mother that he had started dating a girl from his school.

Chesca was incensed when she found out. She always thought Manolo was rude, someone who acted like he was too mature for any of us—and I had to remind her that we were the exact same way, except to other people.

"Well now we know he's a jerk," she said. She was on my side, but I didn't want to hear what she was saying. "You're better off without him."

FOUR

Now

I PUSHED HIM BACK, after an embarrassingly long moment. "Normal people just say hello," I said, wiping my lips with the back of my hand. "How did you know I came back?"

He looked at me, a little amused. "Does it matter?"

"I didn't tell anybody."

"Well, somebody told me."

"Manolo, I left so I could get away from everybody. That includes you. I don't appreciate people I wanted to get away from spying on me."

He searched my face and saw that I wasn't kidding. "I know Anna Lopez's brother."

So it was that easy. He found out where I was staying, discovered a connection, and from there it was a simple step to ask when I had planned to go home.

"Where's your girlfriend?" I said pointedly. Truth was I

didn't know if he had one. Given our history, it was the safer assumption.

"I don't have one."

"Well, I'm behind on news. I didn't check my email at all."

"Fine, Kimmy, if this is how you want it." He sounded frustrated, which was rare. "I just wanted to say that I'm glad you're back. I missed you. Can you just forget the last thing I did to make you mad?"

"Don't even start."

"Well then," he continued, "I dropped by as a favor to Chesca. She asked me to make sure that you'll be at the Country Club for your dress fitting in...well, in thirty minutes."

Chesca asked a favor of Manolo? I didn't believe it.

"When did you start being friends with her?" I asked, suspicious.

"We're not friends," he said, sitting on the chair next to the TV. He always sat there; I never understood why. "But I've been doing some things for her wedding recently and this is just one of those things."

"How long have I been away? She still hates your guts, right?"

He laughed. "Yes, she does, but it doesn't matter. I'm still the best man."

Being away from him that long, I hadn't been able to practice my poker face either. "Are you kidding me?"

"Why are you so surprised? I'm the reason why Andrew and Chesca even know each other."

Andrew and Chesca. They were why I had flown back in that day, why Manolo was in my house, why my mother was very much aware of where I should be. Chesca, my best friend since infancy, was getting married to her boyfriend Andrew on Friday. I was Chesca's maid of honor.

Andrew was Manolo's friend originally; he had introduced them. So he got to be best man.

Manolo checked his watch. "Hurry up before Chesca calls and starts yelling."

"You've forgotten that I can drive."

He blinked at me. "Your mom sold your car. And her car is being fixed. I'm driving both of you to the Country Club today."

"She sold my car?"

"She said she emailed you."

I didn't really *own* that car; it was hers anyway. "I guess I don't have a choice," I said.

Just a few more days, I told myself. *Hang on until the wedding, Kimmy.*

FIVE

My mom and her super-tight barkada from high school stayed in touch for pretty much the rest of their lives. They went to college together, attended each other's weddings, bought homes within ten minutes of one another, sent their kids to the same schools, and joined the same Country Club.

Their three daughters—me, Chesca and Isabel—became the Country Club Princesses (not an official name). It was a second home to us. I spent summers swimming there, playing tennis, studying instruments, and other things to pass the time. And everyone knew who we were. They would address me by name, and knew which table I normally got at the café, what time I used the pool, stuff like that.

My dad was probably still paying for our membership. He was the rich one, and because I decided to stay with my mom I saw our lifestyle gradually become more modest. The latest thing to go was apparently my car, but that was fair. But the Country Club was always there, a reminder that my dad could still be kind. He knew how much my mom's friends meant to her.

One of my earliest memories at the clubhouse was of meeting Chesca. We were probably three years old at the time, although my mom claims that we would be put in a crib together as babies. As a little kid, she was perfectly groomed and dressed, not a hair out of place. I threw an inflatable plastic ball at her face and it got some mud in her eye, and she cried. My mom pulled me away from her quickly and told me not to do that ever again.

***

"LOOK WHO'S BACK!" "How was New York?" "Did I hear right, did you go to Europe?" "You look so pale!" "You've lost so much weight!"

I plastered a smile on my face as I hugged my mom's friends and their husbands. Tried not to roll my eyes as they talked over me, not so much interested in my actual answers to their questions. Yes, New York was fabulous. No, I did not go to Europe. I didn't know why I looked pale. I lost weight because I didn't have any money and didn't splurge on food as much.

They weren't asking me about the breakup at all, so Mom probably gave them a briefing. But then again, that was probably the only thing they talked about for months.

The Country Club's main restaurant was where we all hung out during brunch. It had been a while and I had forgotten how large it was. I'd once been to a party with three hundred guests there, but during brunch it had the familiarity of someone's living room. The large hall opened up onto the garden and outdoor tennis court, and despite being officially the "rainy season," the sun was bright and shiny.

Something else called out to me though. As soon as I was able to slip out, I headed for the buffet table. *Okay, so I do miss this part.* I went straight for the steak station and asked for a big slice, medium rare. Then I scooped some rice and a little mountain of potato salad onto the same plate. I took a seat at our regular table, where Isabel was already at her usual place.

"You *are* alive," she said, blowing me a kiss.

I loved Isabel, genuinely. She was the nicest person.

When we were kids she looked pale and awkward, huge eyeglasses usually trained on a book. She was not the kind of girl I would normally be friends with. In fact, I remembered her being at every party and event with me as a child, but she was just different. She was the "good sister," we liked to say, and Chesca and I were the "evil stepsisters."

The differences weren't as clear anymore. Isabel was probably the most transformed of us. The glasses were gone. The frizzy, unruly hair had been tamed and shaped into a bob. She had a career in real estate, and was apparently a serial monogamist. I swear, she *always* had a new boyfriend, but never brought the same guy to an event twice. She was obviously keeping all of this to herself in high school, and let me and evil Chesca do the acting out.

"So is your new boyfriend in the bathroom or something?" I teased.

"He's in Dubai for work until next week," Isabel informed me. "You'll meet him when he's back."

"I really missed you. No shit."

"I'd believe you more if you actually emailed me."

"Well, you know how I felt at the time. Needed to get a new perspective, and all." It wasn't an excuse, though. I needed to get away, but cutting her off like that wasn't fair. She wasn't involved in that nasty mess in any way. I didn't want to engage in chismis at all, so I just dug into my steak. It tasted fabulous, just melted in my mouth.

"Oh look, the runaway bride is back," a familiar voice said.

A chill crept up my spine. I hated that tone of hers— sarcastic as if on the surface, but I knew that she really meant it.

"Bitch," I said to Chesca, a big smile on my face. "Come here and kiss me."

To her credit, Chesca looked so beautiful right then. Probably the best she had ever looked her whole life. Her skin was flawless. She likely went into a serious diet and exercise regimen for her wedding—she looked like she could lift me and throw me right into my assigned seat if she needed to.

She was wearing the cutest pair of chunky sandals too. They were perfect with her green sundress, which was probably new because I didn't recognize it. For most of our lives we bought clothes together, and we used to know every single item in the other's closet.

"Can you not eat so much? You're going to ruin your measurements. You know how stressful it is for everyone that they're getting to fit you just now?"

"Hello, Kimmy. So glad you made it back in time for my wedding!" I retorted.

We were always like this, so I shouldn't have been surprised. On "bad" days I hated her, and other days I loved her because we were on the exact same wavelength. Today, I could tell, was a bad day. Isabel shot me a look, and I knew that she wanted us to be civil.

So I tried to be civil.

"Where were you last Christmas?" Chesca said, busying herself with taking the table napkin and laying it out on her lap. "We all went to Laiya to stay at Andrew's friend's resort. So much fun."

"I was... I was in Chicago," I said. I remembered not wanting to spend the holidays with relatives I barely knew, so I spent it alone.

"Huh." Chesca grunted, buttering a roll. "Isn't that like a really bad time to go to Chicago? Being so cold and all? That doesn't sound like fun."

I had a great time there, as a matter of fact. But I didn't feel like telling an unenthusiastic audience all about it. "It was fine."

SIX

Then

I HAD A REAL SISTER, flesh and blood, but she decided to live with our dad when our parents separated. We never got along like Chesca and I did. At first I hung out with Chesca because our families were always together, but as pre-teens we became friends by choice.

Chesca and I, like I told Manolo, looked nothing alike. She was naturally slim, and her features were delicate, fair and petite. She looked...*sweet* actually, which was why people would mistake her for a nice girl. I was taller, my hips filled out a bit more, the shape of my eyes and jawline sharper, my dark hair and eyes dramatically contrasting with my skin. We'd gone to parties together dressed as an angel and a witch (guess which one I was), and that was always a hit with people.

In grade five, we saw one of our classmates bring a sheet of colorful, glittery stickers to school. She wasn't even making a big deal out of it, and there wasn't anything super special about them, but we saw the pretty. I caught Chesca's eye, and without planning or talking, we immediately approached her and tag-teamed the poor girl into giving *us* her stickers.

We succeeded too. I lost most of my share within a week.

Chesca was my friend because she understood how I thought, a bit too much, because she was the same way. You were better off with that person as your friend, than anything else.

In high school we got even worse, because we had more girls to practice on. If you went to school with us, you would think that Chesca and I had a lot of friends—but really, it was just us. We let one girl join our "group" because she had a driver and her own car. Another because she was good at math and she let Chesca copy off her once. We also kicked people out of our group fairly regularly, if and when they stopped being useful, so yeah, we weren't very nice.

And this was how we did it: Chesca invited the girl into the group, and *I* eventually did something to kick her out. But we made decisions together, and just played different roles. She was always the angel, and I was always the witch.

In what seemed like a lifetime ago, I cared about Chesca enough to ask her to be my maid of honor. Obviously my judgment was severely impaired.

Maybe it was me, maybe every decision I made was on the wrong side of things. My own wedding planning was more chaotic, the fitting of my own dress included. Julian, a dear friend from college and up-and-coming designer, did my wedding dress. As well as my mom's, and Chesca's, and the bridesmaids'. I only had six months to prepare for my day so I was lucky that he had spared the time, but oh the fights we had. He was "artistic," I was "opinionated," and we would yell at each other, but afterward we would hug and watch an old episode of *Sex and the City* or something.

I never got to see the finished wedding dress, by the way. It was delivered to my house in the grand big box the day after Zack called the whole thing off. My mom quickly hid it, and to my knowledge the most beautiful dress I owned was under a bed somewhere.

By now I could say I was over it, but that little detail still made my head hurt.

SEVEN

Now

CHESCA'S FITTING was a lot less stressful. In fact, all I had to do was show up. The dress she selected for me was a beautiful strapless gown in heavy chiffon, the color of red brick, and they only needed to adjust the hemline to match the shoes I was going to wear.

"How come you still know my size?" I said, twirling around in front of the mirror they brought. "You haven't seen me in a year."

Chesca marked a piece of paper and slipped it into a clear book. "I guessed. You were probably at your fattest six months ago, because you would have still been stress-eating. But you would know that you had to show up this week, so you'd get your ass back in shape. Oh, and you're going to have to work off the huge steak you just ate."

Wow, same old Chesca. She said it so matter-of-factly, and almost coldly, that I twirled around again just so I wouldn't have to look at her. Maybe she was going through the motions too, like dealing with me as her maid of honor was just another item on her checklist. We had been in the Country Club for hours and she hadn't once asked me, like *really asked me*, how I was doing. She wasn't telling me about the wedding either. In fact, throughout the fitting she just sat there, flipping through the damn clear book.

As soon as they took the dress off me, Chesca sat me down in front of a mirror while she and her stylist Lucy hovered over my head and discussed my hair and makeup.

"I think we should keep her hair down," the bride said, as if I weren't in the room.

Lucy twirled a lock of my hair around her finger and laid it down gently on my shoulder. "But we pin it back, like just a little behind the ears?"

"Yes. You have the hair accessory I gave you, right?"

"Should it go here in the middle or off to the side?"

"Slightly off center, I think."

"Won't that make my head tip over?" I said, knowing that it didn't matter anyway.

They barely looked at me to acknowledge what I'd said, and then started testing shades of foundation and lipstick on my face. I played the dutiful mannequin and shut up, and instead used the time to think.

I didn't just return to Manila for her wedding, although Chesca would likely take credit for it. I came back because I was reclaiming the life I had run away from. Sure, it was a life that was a shambles presently, but my year of feeling sorry for myself was over.

Lucy worked on my face quickly. Chesca decided that the palette was a little too dark, but overall it was fine.

"Just take it down a bit on Friday," she said. "I want something rosier but less red."

"Are we done?" I said. "I have something important to do."

That got her to notice me, the person in the dress. "What? I thought your mom said you didn't have anything to do but help with wedding stuff!"

"My mother doesn't handle my schedule. Why, what should I be doing?"

The clear book pages flipped quickly, and with precision. "Despedida de soltera at our house tonight. Starts at six p.m. You shouldn't just go off and miss *that*."

"That's four hours from now. I've got enough time."

Chesca stood up and I could have sworn I heard her wheezing. "Where are you going?"

"You don't handle my schedule either."

"Yes I do because you *keep disappearing on me*. Take Manolo with you if you're going anywhere."

That was odd. When did Manolo become her errand guy? "I'll take Isabel."

"It's Tuesday. Isabel has to work. Take Manolo, I'm sure he's willing to skip work for you. Why are you being so difficult?"

"Why are you being Little Miss Dictator? I'm asking Isabel. See you tonight."

EIGHT

When I was sleeping on couches, futons, and guest bedrooms for a year, I started to appreciate the idea of having my own space. I was charmed by my cousin's IKEA storage setup, my friend's new curtains, my aunt's cherry-blossom-theme guest room. By the end of it I felt like I had cut off my attachment to my house, or at least the idea that home was only ever going to be one place.

This one-bedroom apartment that Isabel showed me, on the eighth floor of a building just at the edge of Bonifacio Global City's business district, looked like a space I could really *be* in. Maybe it could be home, at least for now?

I managed to get Isabel to skip work and join me that afternoon. I told her I wanted a new apartment in Bonifacio, and that it had to be a short walk from my former office's new building, and we only had four hours to find me a new place to live.

"I'll take it," I told her, as soon as I walked into the bathroom and found it surprisingly spacious (relatively) and clean.

"Kimberly!" Isabel scolded from the kitchen. "You don't say yes to the first thing you see!"

Oh, but I did that, all the time. I went for things that felt right, and sometimes the first apartment was the right one. From the second we walked in, I felt good about the place. For one, it was already somewhat furnished. There was a bed, a television, a couch, a refrigerator, air-conditioning for the bedroom. The broker said something about it being recently "freshened up"—a fresh coat of off-white paint, new light bulbs, new cabinets—and I wanted it right away. He stepped out to ask the building manager something, and I pretty much wanted to sign a lease contract then and there.

The plain white appealed to me. It was like a clean slate.

"I don't care," I said, letting myself out onto the little balcony. "Can you arrange it so I can move in this weekend?"

"What the—? Don't you want to see just one other place? To compare."

"No, this is good. I don't want to waste time. And why would you even show me something I wouldn't want to get?"

Despite this being a bit too impulsive for her taste, Isabel got it done. In a few hours, I had a lease on the place for a year, including a guy with a truck coming over in a few days to pick up my stuff. Isabel had advanced the required payments, which I promised to reimburse within the next two months.

On my long "vacation," I stayed with people who hadn't seen me in years, and I didn't get any grief from them about things I should be doing, shouldn't be doing, shouldn't have done. No baggage. It was a wonderful way to live.

When I had the epiphany telling me to go home, I knew that I had to keep that feeling alive for as long as I could.

The practical way to do that was to avoid people who *did* give me grief about everything.

Isabel was *not* one of those people. I grew up with her but I didn't see enough of her, especially since she went to a different college and hung out with a totally different crowd once she started working. But she was always there for me, and I knew that I needed her help if I was going to go through with this.

NINE

Then

ISABEL and I became close only in high school. We went on a family trip together and Isabel started talking about what she had been reading, and she lent me a copy of *Othello*.

I wasn't dumb, by the way. I *read*, sure, teen romances and mysteries, but I was stuck with boring people in a boring place, and I must have been in the mood for Shakespeare that day. Turned out, I really enjoyed it. I actually sought Sab out after dinner and asked her if I understood it right, and she seemed pleased that I was genuinely interested.

We talked until our respective families ushered us back in our cars. I found out more about her, and even though we didn't have much in common, she seemed to really listen to what I had to say. That was surprising, because in high school Chesca and I hung out with people who were more like us. Or at least had something we needed.

"Do you talk to Chesca like this?" I asked her then. "I mean, like all night? Talking about everything?"

"Yeah, we do," Isabel said, shrugging. "You're both really interesting when you're...separate."

I laughed. "Together we're what?"

She didn't answer, but she raised an eyebrow.

Later that year I decided to write a term paper on *Othello*. I didn't even ask Isabel to write entire parts of it. I wrote it myself, incorporating what I thought at the time was super brilliant analysis of Iago being like those girls in high school, the kind you stayed friends with for some reason but should never really trust. I gave Isabel a copy with a note, telling her how much I appreciated our "Othello talk" that night.

A few days later I got sent to the principal's office. They suspected that I didn't write my paper, and wanted me to admit it. And then, within the same afternoon, I got sent back there again—and the principal apologized to me.

"We have it on good authority that you did write the paper yourself, Kimberly. We're sorry for doubting you."

"Um... thanks." I knew this was the time to be eloquent, just to prove that I really *could* write, but I didn't know what to say. I'd been in the principal's office before, sometimes with the nun who handed out discipline cards, and *that* was scary. But having them apologize to me? That was just confusing.

"How did you do it?" I asked Isabel that Sunday, when I saw her at brunch.

She knew right away what I was talking about. "I'm friends with Ms. Herrera and she asked me if I wrote this paper for you. I said I lent you my book and we talked about it, but that you wrote it on your own."

"And she believed you?"

"Of course." Because Isabel didn't get in trouble, didn't lie for the heck of it. Ah, people with integrity. They could get away with so much.

I impulsively hugged her. "Thank you."

TEN

Now

"SO WHAT ARE you up to, Kimmy?" Isabel asked me, eyes darting skeptically.

"There," I pointed to a space to park on the street where Chesca's family lived. "Why do you think I'm up to something?"

"Does Tita Erica know you're moving out?"

No, I hadn't exactly told my mother yet. "She'll find out soon."

"Why are you moving out? You know that it's only her in the house now, right? Your Yaya Moning went back to the province. My cleaning lady comes over to your house once a week."

I knew *that*. Yaya Moning was a part of my household since I was born, and the story of her leaving was told in a long email from my mom. Which I didn't reply to.

"Mom and I will appreciate each other more if we just

see each other on weekends. Trust me, we both know this is true."

"Are you depressed?" Successful at parking, she pulled at the hand brake and turned to me to tap my forehead. "I mean, do you still need to talk? You were away for so long. I only knew you were alive because someone would tell me that they saw you somewhere."

"I gave my mother regular updates, come on. It's not like that."

Isabel shook her head. "For you? I used to run into you everywhere. I always knew where you were. Not knowing if you were okay was weird."

She emailed me, often at first. In the first month I still checked my email, and Isabel wrote lengthy letters telling me the things she would have told me over dinner. At first I wanted to reply, but kept putting it off.

Then I got used to just *not* logging on. The message backlog piled up, until there were hundreds of unread emails waiting for me, and it became easier to not read them at all. She also started emailing less, and I wasn't sure who gave up first.

"Well, I'm here now," I said. "And I'm seriously back. I have a plan and everything. By the time I move into that apartment, my life will be shiny and new. You don't have to worry about me anymore."

Chesca's family lived in a beautiful home five minutes from the Country Club, the same house they'd lived in for as long as I'd known them. Tita Chat, Chesca's mom, was a "frustrated architect" and over the years built and rebuilt their home according to the trends of the day, and her mood. This incarnation of their house was Santorini-inspired, and since Isabel and I were forty minutes late, the party was already in full swing.

Isabel stopped me and gave me her Skeptical Face one last time before we went in. "So the Zack drama is over? You're fine?"

"Yes," I answered firmly. "If you don't believe anything I say, at least believe that I am really, truly, totally over Zack."

The despedida de soltera is a gathering, usually a dinner party, hosted by the bride's family. They invite their relatives, cousins, cousins of cousins sometimes, everyone's significant others, as well as the groom's family and their own clan. In many cases it's probably the first time that both families are together in the same place. I guess nowadays it's held as close as possible to the day of the wedding, so that the aunts, uncles and cousins flying in from abroad can make it. Practically every Filipino family has an aunt or uncle living outside of the country. That's just how it is.

My wedding was called off nine days before the day itself, so I didn't get to have a despedida de soltera. None of the invited out-of-towners were in town yet.

Not that I'm bitter or anything.

As soon as Isabel and I walked in, heads turned. I tried not to notice that half the people at the party were also supposed to have been my wedding guests, but it was difficult. I felt like I was walking into one of those dreams I used to have, dreams about going to my own wedding over and over and it would be slightly different each time.

"Pilates," I yelled into the suddenly silent foyer full of people. "That's why I'm so thin. I know what you're all thinking!"

People giggled, and nodded, and returned to their conversations with relief, and I shoved a shrimp canapé in my mouth and hoped that I sounded like myself again.

"IT'S NOT POSSIBLE. How can you survive?"

I shrugged. "You get used to it. I can't believe I'm telling you this, Tita Chat. You never use your cellphone! But don't worry, I'm getting a new one on Monday."

Two hours later and I was having the tenth version of this conversation. I would tell people that I was back for good, and they would ask for my cellphone number, and then look shocked—*shocked*—when I declared that I didn't have one. I hadn't had my own phone for six months.

My mom had my old one disconnected, I suppose, when it became clear to her that I was serious about not using it. I got by borrowing phones from the people I stayed with, using disposable prepaid SIMs and learning how to use pay phones again. I just figured that if someone really urgently needed to reach me, all they had to do was call one person—the one I happened to be staying with. No one really did that but my mother, a few times. And my so-called best friend, to tell me when I had to be home.

"I'm glad you're back," Chesca's mom said, hugging me. "Chesca's been so stressed out, handling all of the wedding stuff on her own."

"Oh she seems like she's got it all under control. I saw her clear book."

"Don't believe that. She would never admit it to me, anyway. Try to help her out if you can, okay?"

That was typical. Chesca never showed any vulnerability, never asked for help. It took a lot for her to call me about her wedding, and I could sense her panic when she realized she couldn't make me come home in time, if I didn't want to.

"I will, Tita," I said diplomatically.

Dinner was served buffet style, and it was a modest spread, at least for Chesca's family's standards. A small lechon, served only one way. Tita Chat's famous spinach lasagna. Pumpkin soup, fish fingers with honey mustard, grilled vegetable kebabs. Two kinds of beef stews. Not exactly thematic in terms of menu.

Oh wait. They're all of Chesca's favorites.

"I can't believe we're eating lechon again. These past two weeks have been a cholesterol fest!"

Apparently I had been lost in my thoughts, just staring at the food, because hearing that from Chesca's cousins beside me jolted me into putting something on my plate. They looked at me, and I smiled back, but they just grabbed their food and left. A little too quickly, like they were uncomfortable around me. Or maybe I was just paranoid.

I forced a smile, at no one in particular, and braced myself for a long night.

ELEVEN

Wednesday
Family photo shoot
Dinner with the Chavezes

THE DESPEDIDA DE soltera wasn't that unpleasant, in the end. I had a good meal, Isabel kept me company, Manolo's friends were there so he wasn't annoying me, and Chesca managed not to say anything passive-aggressive so we were actually civil to each other. It put me in a good mood and I woke up the next morning feeling ready for my next challenge.

I had an appointment at ten-thirty a.m., at my former office. I was going to try to get my job back.

Consider me super serious about reclaiming my life. A week before, I made an overseas phone call to the head of Human Resources and said I was going to be back in town. A long time ago he had said to me that I could come back if I wanted to, and I was going to take him up on that offer. I hoped he was sincere.

Getting from my mom's house to Bonifacio Global City, the business district where my office was now based, was tricky. I didn't have a car, and cabs were notoriously uncooperative in this part of town. Then again I shouldn't have worried, because as soon as I was out the door I caught Manolo's car pulling over.

"Where are you going?"

"What are you doing here? Don't you have work?"

"Best man duties," Manolo shrugged. "Where are you going?"

"To the corner to get a cab."

"You're kidding, right? Get in the car."

"I haven't told you where I'm going."

He rolled his eyes. "Where are you going?"

"Bonifacio."

"I'll drive you. Get in the car."

"I'm sure I can get a cab."

"Kimmy, when someone does something nice for you, just say thank you."

It was probably going to be hard to get a cab, and I didn't want to be late for my Please Give Me My Job Back meeting. So I got in the car.

I USED to rule my office.

It was my first real job, straight out of college. I got into a management trainee program at a major consumer goods company and I *rocked* it. Six months, I told myself, was enough time to figure things out, and I was right. By my first year I was consistently the best in my batch, according to various evaluations, and yes—people started hating me.

What did I do? That would depend, again, on people

you asked. According to Ramon, also a trainee, I stole a business trip to Hong Kong from him. I say, he was never going to get it to begin with—it was part of a project *I* had been working on for three months. He came in two weeks before the trip and expected to be sent there anyway? With what, all of my notes?

According to Merlie, assistant manager of the PR department, I unfairly took over an internet campaign from her and cost her a promotion, which hurt her so much that she quit. I say, her "campaign" was composed of a couple of press release (full of errors!) and a list of email contacts. Good thing I caught it before it went out, otherwise her own team would have had to spend months winning back good will.

According to Marjorie, another trainee at the time, I stole her boyfriend. That somehow I had manipulated the trainee system so that Zachary Tomas and I would be paired up on provincial trips together, and on one of those trips I apparently seduced him. I say, those provincial trips weren't random. They were trips that *the two best trainees* were sent to, and Zack and I were the best.

I didn't know for sure where the new office was, only that they had recently transferred to this one from Makati. Manolo was familiar with the area and not only dropped me off, he even gave me one of his phones (he had three) so I could call and let him know when I was done. Thankfully it was the simplest phone he had, one that could only call and text, because I couldn't figure out how to work the newer models.

At least I didn't have to swallow my pride in vain. When I got there, HR Manager Harvey was all smiles.

"Welcome back, Kimmy," he said. "You can start on Monday."

It took me about ten seconds to understand what just happened. "Wait," I said, uncharacteristically humble. "I came here to be interviewed. I practiced and everything."

"You don't have to. You were one of the best in your batch."

"That's it?" My voice never squeaked, but it might have a little right then.

"No, that's not *it*," Harvey said. "You'll have the same job title. And salary. You were away for a year, so some of your Management Trainee batchmates are at least one bracket beyond you now."

"But I quit, didn't I?"

"Technically, you went on leave, which all of your managers approved. This doesn't affect your years of service, but you won't get any credit for the time you were away."

Oh my God. Just accept it and stop asking questions! "That's fair," I managed to say. "I'll catch up."

That answer pleased him. "Exactly what I wanted to hear. They're even putting you back in Health and Beauty."

That was the division I used to be in, the division I *ruled*, but for that one incident with a boss who threw me under the bus that meeting. If I was let back in there, my climb back up was going to be easier. I fully expected to be given a tough gig, something totally beyond my comfort zone, like Household Chemicals—but maybe I did at least one good thing in my life after all, to deserve this.

"I have to say," I admitted, "I thought you'd make it more difficult for me."

"I told you then that all you had to do was say you're ready."

"Yes, but that was...I was so messed up then."

What happened was that I left without the customary

month's notice, didn't turn over my workload, didn't clear out my desk. Didn't even shut down my desktop, which that morning had seventy unread emails waiting for me.

"It happens more often than you think," he said. "At your level the pressure can get too much for people, especially if they're going through something personal too. No offense. You might have thought you were different."

"Then thank you, thank you, thank you. I won't let you down this time."

"We have counseling services available if you need them."

I didn't know that, but then again it didn't feel right to have my office pay to sort out the life that they didn't mess up. I had my own way of coping. "Thank you, but my vacation has really recharged me. I'm ready to do this again."

"Good. Go one floor up for a quick orientation, then we'll see you on Monday."

"FUCK ME."

I could have sworn I whispered that, but Marjorie Pineda had ears like a bat. "No thank you," she said, a smirk on her face.

So yeah, I just found out that my new boss was going to be Marjorie Pineda, as in the ex of Zack Tomas, as in the same girl who thought I stole him from her. The universe wasn't letting me off that easy.

"So you're the head of Health and Beauty now?" I said, clearing my throat, trying to keep it civil.

"Yes," Marjorie said, slowly and with much satisfaction. She busied herself with setting up her laptop; I looked down at the wood paneling of the conference table and thought of what to say next.

I didn't seduce Zack the way you think I did. Not exactly on topic.

True, Zack and I were drawn to each other during those provincial trips. At first I thought it was because he was handsome and smart (obviously my type), but later I figured out what it was—we were both hung up on other people, but pretending not to be.

The short story of my non-wedding was that Zack left me for another ex (not Marjorie), one that he had been in love with since high school. What he did to me hurt my pride mostly, but that was not why my mental state deteriorated to the point that I had to leave everything behind.

Once things settled down, I actually understood him. Didn't blame him at all.

I would think that Marjorie would be just as mad at *Zack's other ex*, and not me, but Marjorie's dislike of me ran deeper than being just about a guy. I knew she resented me, because I was better at the job than she was. She and I were hard workers, but she must have been operating under the assumption that attractive girls were somehow inferior.

She wasn't *ugly*, by the way. She just took herself a bit too seriously.

For the next hour I bit my tongue as she explained to me what her plans were for the team, what she had been working on for the past year, and what her goals for me would be. She wanted me to liaise with Public Relations— no problem, could do that with my eyes closed. I could see that my challenge was not going to be the work, but her, if I could trust her with my career. At the end of it I was convinced that they really did think I would be back; the place set aside for me was clear and important.

"Any questions?" she said at the end of her presentation.

A dozen popped into my mind right away. I wanted to know who her direct boss was, so I could make nice to him/her and bypass her entirely. I wanted to know if there were other people in her team with the same rank as me, so I knew who to benchmark against. I wanted to know how long she had been at this position, so I could figure out how much time I needed to catch up to her. And a few other questions that I was sure would make her hate me more.

"No, we're cool," I said, smiling instead. "If I think of any, I'll ask you on Monday."

"See you then," she said, still looking very pleased with herself. "Looking forward to working with you."

MANOLO SURPRISED me by swinging by the lobby of my office building, a mere minute after I texted him that I was done. I knew he offered to drive me, but when was he ever reliable? He came and went as he pleased.

"So you're not working this week at all?" I said as I got into his car.

"Perks of being the child of the owner," he said, maneuvering back onto the road. "It's a slow week for me anyway. Did you get your job back?"

"Yes," I said, letting the relief wash over me. I went in there with perfect posture and my head held high, but I *really* needed that job. Holy crap, this whole reclaiming my life thing would have fallen flat if I had to start over at some mediocre desk job. And my savings had to be replenished ASAP. "I start next week."

"You didn't have to go back there, you know. I could have found you something at my office."

Was he serious? I peeked at him, wondering if this was one of those times when he would say something he didn't really mean, like "See you later."

I decided not to bite. "I'm never working for you again, Manolo."

I knew he was thinking of the same thing. "Well, never say never, Kimmy."

Never, I told myself silently.

"So...is your ex still working there?"

I sighed. "Yes he is."

"Is that going to be a problem for you?"

"No," I said, and I meant it. I had no feelings for Zack anymore. "That's over."

TWELVE

Then

I DID my on-the-job training the summer before senior year in Manolo's dad's company. They imported several brands of luxury cosmetics, and when I asked Tita Mariela for the internship I honestly wanted the marketing experience and, hello, makeup! I thought it would be fun.

I did *not* intend to place myself back in Manolo's life after he stopped calling me when he started college, no matter what Chesca thought of it.

"You won't be able to stay away from him," she predicted, in her know-it-all way that really got to me. "Just sign up for the ad agency with me and maybe we'll have *fun* this summer, instead of you bitching about him all the time."

At the time Manolo was working for the marketing department. Weird, right, having a guy like him work in cosmetics? But no, it was brilliant—good-looking guy sells makeup to girls—and he knew it. He had meetings almost every day, and I "shadowed" him for some of them, quietly taking notes as he worked. And "worked" could also mean "flirted," with beauty editors, and marketing managers, and other women who enjoyed talking to a smart, attractive guy.

Sometimes he would look past them, toward me, and say stupid things like, "Kimberly, were you able to write that down?" Or "Yes, Ms. Lazaro, next time Kimberly won't forget our meeting." And other variations of it, and all I could do was nod and roll my eyes and take notes.

Because I really was there to learn. It was inspiring, actually. That summer I found out that this kind of work was all about making people like you, and my education was in watching a guy work out deals for products he didn't even use.

He had the same charm, but not as cranked up, during the weekly marketing meetings. I watched him present his ideas to the VP (Manolo wasn't the boss yet, which surprised me), and make the effort to say something constructive about everyone else. He could have been blowing hot air but he gave you the impression that you did something great that week.

He also liked to stay behind and tidy up *after every meeting* and one time I actually waited, staying in my seat on the other side of the table as everyone else left the room. For about a minute, I just watched him copy the notes on the white board onto his notebook.

"Why do you do that?" I asked.

He was focused on the board and continued without looking at me. "Notes."

"But you heard what everyone just said. I still remember everything."

"I can't take notes while at the meeting because I'm talking to everybody," Manolo said, still not looking at me. "I have to write everything I remember at the end, before I lose it."

"Oh." I watched his handsome left-side profile in silence for a bit.

I had heard, of course from boastful parents, how smart he was. How much potential he had. I dismissed it as things all parents said, but seeing it in action? Kind of hot. Chesca was half right—an internship with him was a bad idea, because it just made those old feelings resurface. But it was also a good thing, because it was a revelation watching him work.

I wanted to wait for him to finish writing, but I couldn't help it. "But aren't you going to end up running this company anyway?"

That made him pause, and look at me. I think it was the first time I saw him *serious*, even after working with him for a few weeks. "If I thought that way, I wouldn't be working here," Manolo said. "This isn't exactly fun."

I shrugged. "Just asking. I guess I wanted to understand."

"Well, *you* could have taken one of those throwaway internships and not actually work. Why are you here?"

"I like makeup?" I joked. "But you're right. I want to learn something."

"So you didn't just want to be with me?" Just like that, he was Evil Manolo again.

"I don't know," I said, sticking my tongue out at him. "Do I really want to be with a guy who sells mascara? Not really."

The next day, Chesca's prophecy fulfilled itself when Manolo asked me to dinner and we started up again. We kissed in his car (and elsewhere) *after* work; otherwise we were perfectly respectable and we never even held hands during the day.

I didn't tell anybody about it this time, and that was probably a good idea. Because he unceremoniously dumped me again as soon as I went back to school.

Technically, Manolo never *dumped* me. I would just hear from the Country Club grapevine that he had a new girlfriend, and it would often be true. That year, it was a magazine editor. He even brought her to Sunday brunch one time, just to quickly introduce her to his family and apologize that they couldn't stay long, because they were on their way to Tagaytay.

She looked nice, fashionable, intelligent—and mature. I didn't meet her personally, though, because I was wearing shorts and had just come out of playing badminton, and I felt like such an immature college kid. I hid in the bathroom until they left.

When I came back out Chesca gave me a look, a mixture of I-told-you-so and pity, always a horrible combination.

THIRTEEN

Now

MANOLO WAS DRIVING, so he didn't pick up the phone when it rang. Or he just saw from the caller ID that it was Chesca and just handed it to me immediately.

"What?" I said, without a hello.

Chesca didn't even sound surprised. "Kimmy, the photo shoot's been moved up. Come over to the Country Club and wear something nice."

"What photo shoot?"

"They didn't tell you? Pre-wedding photo shoot with my entourage! Wear something nice! The photographers are already here! Where are you?"

"Did you know we had a photo shoot today?" I asked Manolo.

He checked his watch. "Isn't that at five?"

"Why do all of you know this and I don't?"

"Tell him to wear something nice and get over here *now!*"

Manolo snickered. "I heard that."

He dropped me off at my mom's house so I could change, and said he'd be back in twenty minutes. Sure, Tita Mariela lived like minutes away from us, but no way was I going to be ready in a "something nice" in that time.

"Take your time." I said.

As I pored over the clothing choices in my closet, I tried to remember if I had a "pre-wedding photo shoot" back then. No, I didn't. Photo shoots were Chesca's thing; she loved dressing up and being photographed professionally. The angel and witch photo we had from Halloween was just one of a series of costumes, formal dress occasions, and faux modeling sessions we did every year. She picked the photographers, planned our poses, and kept prints of everything in the volumes of scrapbooks that lined her bookshelf.

One last photo shoot for old times' sake then, I thought, and picked out one of my nicer dresses.

SHIT.

For all my drama about how I needed to stay away from Manolo for my own mental health, I had to admit: We looked *good* together.

I saw our reflection on the mirror near the front door of my mom's house as we left, and it became obvious to me again, with extra strength this time. He looked even better now, at thirty, than he did at eighteen. Back then he was a bit on the lanky side, but now he had grown into a shape similar to that of his dad and the other men in his family. Tall. Sturdy. That black shirt he was wearing was cut perfectly for his body. Dressing in a way that affected me was something he always knew how to do.

Black looked good on me too, and we had a moment when I got back to the living room and saw him waiting for me, sitting again on that same chair.

Manolo stood up, and I saw where his eyes were going. He took it all in, from my neckline down to my toes, and my disobedient heart skipped a beat.

"Dude," I said, snapping my fingers. "Eyes up here. My hair looks great, don't you think?"

"Yeah, that too," he said, smiling slyly.

Chesca was not as happy to find out that the best man and the maid of honor wore black to her Pre-Wedding Photo Shoot.

"Why would you do this to me?" she wailed, but it was rhetorical. "You know the theme is Ivy and Brick."

"You didn't say we had to follow a theme!" I said.

"Yeah but *black*? Really? Who wears black to a wedding-related *anything*?"

I didn't know the theme of her wedding was Ivy and Brick. So that was why my maid-of-honor dress was that strange but lovely color. I wanted to ask her why she chose it, but then I remembered—her old house.

Tita Chat's constant rebuilding of their house was something Chesca didn't enjoy. She hated the process of packing up her things again, and then moving back into the same room, except it looked entirely different. Her favorite version of their home was the first one, the one that had a façade of red bricks and some wild vine crawling up one wall. That was almost completely remodeled into something else when we were seven years old.

What was my theme again? Coral. Chesca's maid of honor dress was in that color and she hated it. I laughed and told her she was overreacting.

The first set of photos was of the bride and groom, and

Chesca looked glowing in her green sundress. She and Andrew starting dating when she was a college senior, spending time apart only during "breakups" that didn't last.

Sometimes it amazed me how Chesca could do it. I knew her secrets, her mean streak, her capacity for cruelty, and yet she managed to have a functional relationship with a guy who absolutely adored her. And because with this crowd it was hard to hide anything, Andrew knew about her past too—that she was a bully, she cheated on tests, lied with a smile on her face when it served her purpose. Maybe the relationship even made her better, because it had been a while since Chesca had been mean or difficult to anyone but me.

That, I realized as I watched her be photographed with her husband-to-be, was why she was better off than me now. Even if we started at the same place. She and I competed often, but she had never been attracted to Manolo.

"Where's the maid of honor and best man?" I heard the photographer say.

Manolo and I walked over, somber people in black next to the happy couple. I pulled out happy thoughts so I could smile for the camera.

FOURTEEN

Then

WHEN WE WERE TEENAGERS, Chesca and I liked a lot of the same things, but we got them in different ways. While I liked to ask for them, Chesca liked to receive them. How do you receive something you never asked for? You set up the situation so that the thing you want is given to you. You know when you're playing chess against someone who makes weird, random moves, and then traps you in the end? That was Chesca.

In contrast, I was loud and obvious, and people didn't like that.

Chesca wished I were more like her. For example, back in high school, she never *ordered* Mellie Chua to do her *Noli Me Tangere* book report for her. But she did find out what subject Mellie was failing at (Home Economics, aka Cross Stitching) and gave her super easy patterns complete with the right color threads, and Mellie was so thankful that she couldn't help but ask what she could do for Chesca.

"Oh, I don't know..." Chesca said, shrugging.

"Do you want me to help you with your English term paper?" Mellie offered.

Chesca shook her head. "No, I'm done with that."

"How about *Noli*?"

"Sure," Chesca said slowly. "But only if you have the time."

Of course Mellie didn't have the time, but she made time for it. That was how Chesca got people to do what she wanted. Effective, but I always found it so tiresome.

When she saw the effect Manolo had on me, she unilaterally decided that she was going to help me out of it.

"You deserve better, are you kidding me?" Chesca kept saying.

I did eventually try to move on, and date other guys, and Chesca was always so ultra-enthusiastic about it. When I was a senior in college, I brought a "boyfriend" to the Country Club brunch for the first time. He was a little older than me, taking a master's degree in literature at the same college.

Chesca had high hopes for us, until she saw how he acted at the brunch. It became a pattern with the guys I brought over. For one reason or another, they didn't like meeting the Country Club people. To them we were snobs, but we just had no patience for the insecure. If we sensed a lack of confidence in someone, most of us didn't even bother to make conversation.

Only Isabel was polite enough to always try to talk to those guys, and I brought some characters over the years. The guy I met at someone's birthday party. The know-it-all law student. The really shy male model. Plus others who were less memorable. None of them deserved to meet my family, and Chesca called me out on that.

During a birthday get-together for Isabel, when I was twenty-two years old and had brought the third random guy to a brunch already, Chesca took me aside.

"You're just bringing them to get Manolo to react," she said. "Get over it, please. It's pathetic."

In the same time span, Chesca had started working at an advertising agency. She was an account executive, and her control freak streak was serving her well. But I was rocking my job too, so she fixated on "helping" with my boyfriend situation, which was, I admit, in shambles.

"Manolo has nothing to do with anything," I said defensively.

"I don't believe you," she declared. "He's only toying with your feelings because you let him. Don't let him."

The annoying thing? Chesca was right. If she were wrong, I wouldn't have hated her so much when she was being all "tough love" toward me.

I did bring those guys to brunch, even those I'd only known a few weeks, just to see what Manolo would do when I introduced them. Sometimes *he'd* be there with the latest girlfriend, and he would politely come up to us and shake the guy's hand. But he always had that look on his face, like in those two seconds they had dueled and he won. I knew it was wrong, but I'd lose interest in the guy soon after that.

Meeting Zack Tomas, though, made Chesca get off my back for once. Because he wasn't a disposable guy. I was getting sick of my string of non-relationships, and he had just broken up with Marjorie.

One night we just said, yeah, screw our lives, we should just start dating.

The experience was strange to me, because I actually *acted* like a real girlfriend, for the first time. Not that I was any good at it. When I brought him to the Country Club, it was because I genuinely wanted my family and friends to meet him. I knew he'd fit right in and be able to talk to anyone else there.

Chesca just loved him. She loved the idea that I had found a guy who could actually keep up with me. I had to explain to him that my best friend was happy in her relationship and did *not* have the hots for him, and that he should just ignore the way she followed him around every night, asking a zillion questions.

Zack was the first guy that was—and I admit it—good enough competition for Manolo. He was good-looking, successful, and not at all afraid of me. When I introduced them both, I had the pleasure of seeing Manolo *not* look smug. He knew this could lead somewhere.

Chesca knew this too, and it made her *so* happy. She was determined that I not "fuck this up." Our friendship at the time was the most conflict-free as it ever had been, because I, too, didn't want to ruin it for myself. I, too, thought I deserved to be happy.

The problem was me, because I didn't know how to be with a good guy. Chesca was all too willing to teach me how.

"Have you met his family?" she demanded.

"No," I said. "I don't think they even know we're together."

"Zack is not like those 'himbos' you've been seeing. He's got a family that he's close to; please show some interest in them."

But I didn't do well with parents of boyfriends. Or female family members of boyfriends. They didn't like me. I was never rude, but they didn't like me anyway. I tried to put off the family thing for as long as I could, always. Probably why every "relationship" I had always ended with me disappearing.

Turned out that I didn't need to do that for Zack. Something was happening in his life at the same time, and we both got caught up in it. He started reconnecting with an old flame, the girl he never forgot. I even met her once, at a party for a common friend, and after being introduced to her I knew that she still loved him too.

I wondered if any of Manolo's girlfriends, those I met in person, were able to say the same about me. Eventually I perfected the art of shaking their hands and acting like I didn't want to strangle them, but could they tell how I felt about him? Was I that obvious? It was very obvious to Chesca. I couldn't hide anything from her.

So, I thought, might as well confide in her. I told her about meeting Zack's ex, and that I was threatened by her, and this put her fussy Alpha Female on panic mode.

"Kimmy!" she yelled. "You have to fight for him! If he's the one for you, you can't let this happen! You know he's going to be really good for you. You can't let him get away."

I knew she was right. I also felt that Zack was a guy I didn't deserve, and that weakness meant I didn't stand up to her when she persuaded me to do something I shouldn't have done.

I proposed marriage to Zack.

He said yes.

IT'S ALREADY BEEN ESTABLISHED that the wedding didn't happen. I was angry when Zack told me that he couldn't go through with it. I plotted ways to get back at the people who helped him reach that decision, but I eventually did accept that it was the right thing to do. Because Zack was obviously in love with someone else.

And so was I.

So the cause of my pain, really, wasn't that my wedding was called off. It was that I was pressured into having one with the wrong person to begin with. Convinced by someone who was my friend, but never let me just be myself, make my own mistakes.

She meant well, but she was why I was a mess. Maybe the simple explanation was that we were no longer as similar as we used to be.

After the wedding on Friday, and upon moving into my new apartment, I was going to take one step toward peace of mind and limit my exposure to certain people. No more Country Club brunches and dinner parties, where people gossiped and schemed. When I got a new phone I would rebuild my contact list carefully, making sure that I stayed in touch with only those I needed in my life.

Who were these people? My mother. Isabel.

How about the Best Friend who made my life miserable? And the First Love who kept coming back with new ways to torment me?

A normal, well-adjusted person wouldn't have those in her life, would she?

FIFTEEN

Now

NEXT ON CHESCA and Andrew's wedding schedule was dinner, hosted by Andrew's family. It was going to be at Eastwood City up north (everything beyond the tollway to the metro center was "north"), and again I needed transportation.

"I have a product launch at four," Manolo said. "Why don't you join me? We can just go to Eastwood from there."

Normally I loved going to those things, especially if I had to for work, but I just got my job back that morning. And found out that someone who hated me was going to be my boss. Too soon to get back in there?

"I don't think so. I mean, I haven't really adjusted to life back here..."

"What, you've gone soft? You know that you're going to have to see these people again anyway. Might as well get it over with."

He knew of course that the way to get to me to do something was to insinuate that I wasn't brave enough to do it. He was right, too. Hiding from these people for another day wasn't going to make me feel any better.

So I went to the product launch with him.

The only thing hotter than Manolo in black was Manolo in black *at work*. He had his own share of admirers because he just looked good, but that was doing a disservice to the fact that he also spoke well and listened like he meant it. When we got to the hotel venue, late of course but in time for cocktails and schmoozing, I saw him put that face on. He was flirtatious without ever seeming unprofessional, and made people think like he was *so* interested in what they were saying. I was first introduced to this side of him when I was an intern, but now I saw even more confidence.

More people, I knew, were falling for it this time. I was always a sucker for a guy who knew what he was doing. In the span of a minute I had about ten fantasies of taking that shirt off him, so I popped a California roll into my mouth and forced myself to think of work.

I had been away for a while and probably needed a warm-up. So the first chance I got, I separated from him and worked the room, introducing myself, and apologizing to people whose calls or emails I didn't return for a year.

"You look great!" "I heard you were in Europe?" "How was New York?" "Call me when you're back at work!"

The society I was brought up in has told me all my life that I should have more shame, but shame was overrated. If I had more of it I couldn't have gone back to Manila at all, or faced my friends and family, or my employer. That meant I would have spent the next stage of my life as a coward, and I used to bully girls for being cowards. I sure didn't want to be one at twenty-seven.

About a third of the people at this product launch I had

worked with in one way or another before, and no doubt knew why I had suddenly dropped out of circulation. Sure, being left at the altar was humiliating, but I had been the subject of rumors before.

My strategy was not to avoid it, but to seem so very over it.

"I just got burned out, you know? Needed to get away and find myself," I said to the first person.

"It was so enlightening, seriously. I was living out of one bag for a long time and realized that I didn't need all of this crap," I told the next person.

By the fifth or so person, I managed to describe my year away as some sort of New Age-y retreat, and maybe I was even starting to believe it.

Eventually I found myself talking to someone I actually liked and respected. Farrah, a beauty editor at a teen magazine, squealed when she saw me and I felt like I could finally relax. "Did you arrive with Manolo?" she said. "I think everyone saw the two of you come in together."

"Yeah." I tried to make it sound casual. "Long story, but he's driving me around for now."

"So this means you're playing in our little sandbox again?"

"You know it," I said, accepting a glass of white wine from the waiter. "What's changed around here? And is it me or is everyone *young*?"

Farrah rolled her eyes. "I know, right? As if I don't feel like such a matrona at my own job already."

Together we walked to a free table where we could set our drinks down, and managed to catch a glimpse of Manolo chatting up four women from a very well-known chain of salons. Farrah bit her lip and pinched my arm.

"Dear God, woman. Look at him. Did he do something recently? Lift weights or something? Why is he so hot?"

"Genetics," I said, faking nonchalance. "Have you seen his relatives? He's the plain one." Not true, but it sounded like something I would say.

"If I were into the random event hookup, I would totally hit that."

And there it was—the familiar pain. "What does that mean?"

Farrah looked left and right and lowered her voice when she spoke. "Well, there was this girl who worked with us for a few months, she used to date him. Talked about him every day, Manolo said this, Manolo was wearing that. So annoying. And then—she just started crying to me. Every day. For three weeks."

"Let me guess. She found out that he was calling someone else his girlfriend."

"More of, she found out that he had slept with someone else. I of course warned her that three dates with Manolo doesn't mean anything, that she shouldn't go around calling him her boyfriend. It was unbelievably pathetic."

Yes it was. Of all people, I knew that best. So he was still that kind of guy.

Why did it hurt? It wasn't like he said he had changed, or that he wanted me again. Sure he was back in my life, only because of Chesca's wedding, and as soon as it was over he would disappear again. Every time he wandered back to my house or the Country Club and deigned to talk to me I stupidly thought that it would be different.

"Well, that's Manolo," I managed to say, despite my mouth drawn into a thin line.

Farrah shrugged. "It's because he's so...luscious," she

said. "Someone needs to break his heart. It's going to teach him how to do this right. Didn't you have a thing with him?"

I coughed. "A long time ago. I'm not the teaching kind though."

From across the room, Manolo saw me looking at him and he smiled. It was not the smile that he used on his work face; it was from the Manolo I knew, that he had briefly slipped back into for my benefit. It was almost like a secret message, because he knew I had my game face on too in front of all of these work people. This was our world, and we were good at it, because we were both shameless. We at least understood that about each other.

LATER THAT NIGHT, Andrew's family returned the favor and bought dinner for Chesca's family. Naturally, this included the Country Club group, because we were family too. It was at a new strip of restaurants in Eastwood, and when we got there I noticed that it was a smaller group than the despedida de soltera of the night before.

Which was fine, because I didn't know that a dinner hosted by the groom's family was part of the wedding planning. I mean, I didn't put that on the schedule for my wedding. I never even met anyone in Zack's family.

These little social missteps were why people hated me. Ah well.

Manolo was in a good mood on the drive over. He was telling me something, apparently good news related to his company, but the conversation with Farrah just shot anything good about my mood.

And yet he seemed so relaxed with me. Whenever he came back into my life he settled in like it was an old chair that was curved to his shape. He was always just as charming, as familiar, and as determined to remind me that he knew how to get under my skin. It was as if he had never done anything to hurt me. That was infuriating, because I remembered everything.

He literally had a chair of that sort in my house, so it wasn't even funny.

I may be shameless, but I can still learn from you. You're way better than me.

Chesca didn't eat much at dinner. Sure she took a token bite or two of the European-Japanese fusion cuisine, but she was hyper aware of her figure and that she was going to be married in two days.

"Remember your dress," she told me as I grabbed a second slice of pizza.

"You'll be a thousand times more photographed than me," I reminded her. "And besides, you'll want to be the fittest, prettiest person there anyway."

I had met the Chavezes (Andrew's family) once or twice before. They were decent people, who lived relatively simple and drama-free lives. As far as I knew, Andrew's only "dark" period was the six months when he thought he was meant to be a career musician. He wasn't very good at it, according to Manolo, and soon embraced the corporate life that he had been trying to avoid.

Since the dinner location was neutral territory, and the guests were more from Andrew's side than Chesca's, *balikbayan* jilted bride Kimmy went mostly unnoticed. I ended up sitting next to my mother, who didn't seem to be wandering off to speak to any of her friends.

It wasn't the most private of situations, but it was probably the best time to mention to my mother that I would be moving out. At the very least she wouldn't cause a scene in front of the Chavez family.

"But that's ridiculous, Kimberly. How will a maid even fit in a one-bedroom?" was what my mom said when I told her. Which was a cringe-fest on several levels because no one said "maid" now but the memo hadn't gotten through to her circle, and even the idea of me needing it, ugh.

Why I had been nervous, I didn't know. I probably thought that she would start crying, that she'd say she would miss me, that she wouldn't know what to do without me. But I already *had* left her alone for the better part of a year.

"I'm not going to have a maid," I said, laughing. "That's kind of the point."

"Oh. Well, your decision then. It's probably for the best because you don't have a car now."

In fact, I shouldn't have been surprised. It was more than ten years now since she and Dad decided to live apart. She wasn't crying over that still; she was obviously enjoying herself. If anything, my moping at home would have brought her down.

My dad now lived in Cebu, which was another place I could have run to last year but didn't. We still spoke sometimes, but I no longer thought of him as the kind of person I went to for help. He and my mom divided my family up equally, and so far we seemed to be satisfied with what we had.

"But Manolo has been driving you wherever you need to go, right?" Mom said, oh so casually as she sliced her fish into tiny slivers.

"Yes, but it's not a good idea."

"Why not?" Mom said innocently. "Manolo visited me a lot when you were away. He was really worried about you."

That was a trick Mom and Tita Mariela played on both

of us, for most of our adult lives, by the way. "Manolo was looking for you"—only for me to show up somewhere, ask him what he wanted, and have to be told that no, he wasn't looking for me.

The thing was? Manolo never came to *me* to ask if I had been looking for him. Even though his mother probably told him the same thing. *Way to make a girl feel special, jerk.*

Ugh. Just remembering that made my blood boil again. After Manolo made me a disposable summer fling twice, the anger became part of my default setting. It was there, simmering in the background, always.

"Just avoid him," Chesca kept saying. *"You're never going to get over it if you keep seeing him like this."*

But I was stupid and couldn't *not* see him, so instead I developed a deeply irritable, snappish, sarcastic personality around him. He did the same for me, and as a result we said some harsh things to each other over the years.

Why my mother never remembered any of that, I didn't know too. But selective memory was probably how she got through the bad times.

SIXTEEN

Thursday
Spa-themed bridal shower
Rehearsal dinner

FOR THE FIRST time in months, I was driving a car.

Pleased to report that driving as a skill came back to me fairly quickly. As soon as I adjusted the driver's seat of Chesca's car (had to push it back because my legs were longer), second nature kicked in and it was like riding that proverbial bike.

What took five more minutes was getting used to the other Metro Manila drivers. A year of being relegated to the backseat of cabs and relatives' cars in other countries made me forget what it was like. It wasn't that they were *faster*, you just couldn't trust them.

As I got onto the tollway from Filinvest, a cab tried to zip into my lane without signaling. I instinctively honked and swore, something I hadn't done in a long time.

"Dick," I added.

Chesca, my lone passenger, blinked at me. "You're driving so slowly now."

"Forgive me if I'm careful on the day before your wedding."

We were on the road just before ten a.m., on the way to a condo unit in Bonifacio for Chesca's bridal shower, hosted by her maid of honor.

Yeah, I was surprised about it too. The maid of honor only found out about it last night, at the end of dinner hosted by the Chavez family, when Isabel pulled me to one side.

"You know what you're doing tomorrow?" she whispered.

"Shopping for a wedding gift?"

"No, you're throwing a bridal shower for Chesca."

"I am?"

She rolled her eyes. "Not really. Chesca told me to tell you, but I knew you wouldn't have enough time to put it all together, so I arranged it. Just take her to this address tomorrow and take credit for everything."

I may have been in the process of cutting off many of my Country Club people, but I was glad that I was keeping Isabel. She worked it out so that all I had to do was drive the bride to the party. Since I didn't have a car, Chesca drove herself over to my mom's house this morning, and then we switched places.

That didn't make sense, but the fact that I was doing this for her mattered to Chesca.

"What kind of spa stuff can we have done?" Chesca asked, excitement creeping into her voice. I was sure she knew, but wanted to pretend that she was the nervous bride who had no idea what was happening.

"Well, no facials or waxing for you, not the day before the wedding," I said. "I think just the massage and foot spa. And some aromatherapy thing."

The shower for Chesca and ten of her closest friends was to be held at a two-bedroom condo in Bonifacio, with massage and mani/pedi services provided by a nearby spa. Chesca wanted it late morning so she wouldn't be rushing to get to the rehearsal dinner. (She loved to take her time with pampering.) Lunch was going to be little fish sandwiches, fruit, and sparkling wine packed by Tita Chat.

"I think you should have your eyebrows threaded," Chesca said bluntly.

"Of course you do."

"It's not a suggestion."

We must have caught the tail end of the northbound rush hour and eventually slowed to a crawl. Suddenly the car seemed so... small. I hadn't been alone with Chesca in a while.

"So what's Andrew up to right now?" I asked, trying to make small talk.

"Nothing. I knew they'd be exhausted from last night so I didn't schedule anything for them this morning. His family, they're not the party types. They're not used to entertaining."

"Not like us, you mean?"

"They're very uncomplicated. Nice people."

I shrugged. "As long as you know where he is."

Chesca gave me a strange look. "I actually told him that he could have a bachelor party, you know, if his friends kidnapped him or something. But if he had sex with anyone there I would make the rest of his life miserable."

I laughed, and was surprised at my own reaction. My own wedding had been called off after Zack's secret bachelor party, planned by his friends. I still wasn't sure what had happened, only that the next day he called me and said that the wedding wouldn't be happening.

But apparently I was over it and could laugh at what Chesca said. Go me.

"That's very mature of you," I said.

She started tapping her feet, and her knees bobbed up and down. It was distracting. "I mean, I'm nervous enough about tomorrow, I don't need to worry about being compared to a professional."

"What are you talking about?"

"Don't give me that. I'm nervous about tomorrow night. I'm not like you."

"I don't get it." And then, I got it. "Wait—you've never done it?"

Chesca winced and then recovered. She had probably prepped herself to admit to her virginity with pride, but I forced her into the defensive. "Yeah, never."

"You've been with him for, what, seven years?"

"Six, if you count the little breakups."

"What were you doing all this time, brushing each other's hair? Why didn't you *tell* me?"

The look on her face didn't just hint at nerves, but an old disappointment as well. "I don't know. I just felt you became so casual about it. I had my reasons to wait, and I didn't want you to talk me out of it."

It was a good thing that I wasn't driving at full speed because this conversation just blew my mind.

"You thought *I* would talk you out of waiting until your wedding night."

"Isn't that what you're implying now?"

"I'm not doing that."

She folded her arms. "I just knew you would. You would tell me that it's nothing, that I should get it over with, and I don't want that. I want this to be special."

I honked absentmindedly at another dick driver and shook my head. "I wouldn't have done that. I wouldn't have trivialized something that important to you. I can't believe you would think that."

"Oh come on," Chesca rolled her eyes. "Don't make this my fault. I just assumed you would."

What exactly about me made people think I was slutty? My outfits? The way I walked, the way I did my hair?

I flirted, sure, but everyone did that. Others weren't so up front about it, and instead flirted by way of contrived situations. You know the type. The girl who would never ask a guy out, but would instead conspire with her friend to hang out in the same place the guy would be in, and pretend to be surprised to see the guy there, and then concoct some reason to continue to talk to him, and then hope that he would call and ask her out.

Marjorie (Zack's ex and my new boss), for example, thought that I stole her boyfriend by setting up provincial trips so we would be alone together. That seemed awfully complicated. If I wanted Zack I would just walk up to him and ask him out. And that was what I did.

(It was very effective.)

Because of that philosophy I went on more dates than a wallflower type of girl, but that didn't mean I was promiscuous. I wasn't surprised that other people weren't smart enough to figure it out, but Chesca? She had known me my whole life.

"What makes you think I slept around?" I demanded, starting to get angry.

"Because I've seen you stick your tongue into the throat of every guy you've ever brought to Country Club brunch! What else was I supposed to think?"

"Don't you think I would have told you about it?"

"Really." This wasn't Chesca just being her usual snappy self. This was actually cold. "Kimmy, have you ever had sex?"

And then I realized that there was no way I could answer that truthfully without revealing even a little bit about That Thing. "Yes."

Chesca sneered, not at all surprised. "When was the first time?"

God why won't these cars move. "About two years ago."

She did the math. "You were with Zack at the time."

"Yes."

As we both sat there, silent, I hoped that she would come to realize that she was wrong about me. Maybe the rest of the world still believed I was a slut, but at least my own best friend wouldn't. Those guys she was talking about? She should appreciate the fact that I didn't just do it with any of them.

"Were you already planning your wedding then?"

Ugh I hate your memory sometimes.

"You were, weren't you? You and I were talking every day. Planning your wedding. Picking out your stupid coral table linens and your pearl white shoes. That would have been a good time for my best friend to tell me if something major happened in her life. But I don't know a thing, apparently. *Why didn't you tell me?*"

Finally, magically, as was usual with South Superhighway, we passed the bottleneck and the road cleared up. I concentrated on just getting us onto C5, and let her question hang in the air. She looked like she didn't need an answer anyway.

I didn't tell her because I couldn't. Maybe I had some shame after all.

SEVENTEEN

Then

THE LAST TIME Marjorie and I worked together was when we were both assigned to the Health and Beauty division of our office two years ago. As management trainees, we were randomly assigned in pairs and deployed to different teams in the company, working there for three months or more until we "graduated" from the program and got absorbed by the divisions that liked us best.

If I didn't quit when I did, I knew I was going to be heading Health and Beauty. But anyway.

We were both sent to a marketing conference, hosted at a swanky hotel. The office even sponsored our stay there throughout the three-day event, and I took it because my house was a long drive away and the sessions started early.

At this time, I was already engaged to Zack, set to marry him in a few months. Marjorie claimed to be totally over him, even had a new boyfriend and everything, but she still hated me. I tried to be nice and made small talk about sharing a room with her, but she curtly told me that no, she would not be staying at the hotel with me.

"Fine," I said. "I offered."

Usually I liked attending these work conferences. I got a chance to practice my schmoozing skills, and some of these people (like Farrah) became good friends. But ever since I got assigned to this department, a knot had formed in my stomach and would not go away. Was it the stress from my upcoming wedding?

On the very first session of the conference, I finally figured out what it was. When Manolo Mella walked in, late, and took the empty seat beside me.

Shit. Of course he would be there. He essentially did the same work for the family business.

Marjorie was sitting on my other side and I didn't dare look at him and say hello. I took notes intently instead, and even tried to have a decent conversation with her, just so I wouldn't have to look at Manolo. But I was fully aware of his presence, and every minute that I ignored him, that he didn't even try to talk to me, my entire right side just burned.

At lunch, Marjorie quickly got out of her chair and muttered that she had to go. She probably wanted to make a quick escape so she wouldn't have to have lunch with me, and I got left with Evil Manolo all on my own.

I sighed and turned to my right, and true enough, he was looking at me, amused.

"Fuck you," I said, shaking my head.

"What?" he said, faux defensive. "I didn't know you'd be here."

"Normal people say hello. Where's your girlfriend?"

He ignored that. "Well, I never really know how to greet you, Kimmy. Last time you slapped me."

Last time, I swatted his arm because he tried to kiss me *as soon as Zack excused himself to go to the bathroom*, but that was typical of him. And me. "This is work, Manolo. We can be civil here at work, right? Don't ruin things for me."

"How would I ruin things for you?"

Just by being here. "Let's just *work*, please?" I said, and against my better judgment I felt that I was starting to beg. "Pretend that we have no history, that we're just colleagues."

"You know me, Kimmy. I'm always professional."

Even the way he said that, the way his voice lingered on "always," the way he moved slightly forward, his finger lightly tapping my knee... agh, what a flirt. Of course, this would be nothing if I weren't pathetic enough to be affected by it.

Think of Zack, think of Zack.

But Manolo was right, he always *was* very professional.

"So, how about lunch?" he said, gesturing for us to stand. "You can introduce me to your officemate."

"She hates me," I said. "She's not going to be hanging out with me here if she doesn't have to."

He smiled, and it had a disarming effect. "Then you're stuck with me."

LUNCH WITH MANOLO was better than I thought it would be. The last time we had seen each other at a work setting was when I was an intern, and it felt good to be dealing with him as equals. Or, more specifically, he was a colleague I admired, and I got to pick his brain about a lot of things that didn't involve "us." That I could be like this with this particular person was not a situation that many could handle. I wasn't like this with other people, and I had to imagine that it was the same for him. This was reserved only for those who could step up, could handle it, could dish it right back.

It was exhausting, but also the most fun you could ever have.

God, why?

We had the option of taking a chicken or fish lunch at the next function room, but Manolo led me to the hotel's best restaurant instead.

"My treat," he said.

"Corporate expense, right?"

"No, it doesn't have to be."

I didn't mind. I didn't want to be seen by my other colleagues with him. He and I were too conspicuous together.

Upon catching up, I learned that he was head of marketing officially. I was surprised, again. I thought by now he'd be a vice president, overseeing not just marketing but other things, but he was serious about learning the ropes.

"This is by choice, right?" I asked. "You want the slow climb up the corporate ladder."

"I'm not going up a ladder," Manolo said, his forehead crinkling up just a little. His age was starting to show, but with it came a bit more...cred? Distinction? "I like to think I'm conquering one summit after another."

"So marketing is not the end of it?"

"No, but it helps get my name around. Otherwise I wouldn't be invited to things like this."

"You're the owner's son. You *will* be invited to things like this."

He bristled at that. "The same way you're invited because you wear short skirts and touch people's elbows when you talk?"

Ha, he'd noticed. "Hey," I protested, "Don't give me that. I learned the corporate flirting from you!"

"I don't 'flirt.'"

"Oh please," I laughed, and then straightened up to do an impression of him. "'Oh Ms. Grace, you really should drop by our office more, we miss your good taste around here' blah blah blah. You play them more than I do."

"You will never hear me admit that." That was probably the closest he came to conceding to me at anything. "You seem to be doing well at work."

"Yes I am," I said, not at all humble about it. "Expect me to be running this division in a few years."

"You're always overly confident," Manolo said, and I thought I detected a hint of warmth there. "It's charming."

"No, it's annoying," I corrected him. "You can't believe how many haters I have at work. Or maybe you can; you worked with me before."

"You never annoyed me."

I was ready to mock him for that, but he was dead serious.

When we returned to the conference, it was as if the lunch hour never happened. We put our "work" faces on and I heard nary a smartass comment from him. Marjorie probably couldn't tell that I even knew who the guy beside me was.

BY THE SECOND DAY, Marjorie made her own friends. She joined them for lunch, and all the coffee breaks, and when the day's sessions ended she said she was having dinner with some of them and we didn't have to hang out together at all.

See, I didn't even *need* to come up with an excuse to avoid her. Marjorie was so efficient that way. I made some new friends too, but Manolo somehow made it a point to always linger nearby.

"Okay, so your officemate really does seem to hate you," he said, approaching after Marjorie dismissed me.

"You thought I was kidding? She thinks I stole her boyfriend. She won't even share the hotel room with me." I laughed softly. "She probably thinks I'm going to stab her in her sleep."

"Yeah right," Manolo said. "She's just an *assistant manager*. It's not worth it."

I laughed from my belly at that, and it felt really good. It wasn't polite to admit it, but being mean together was *fun*. But don't do it, kids.

———

FOR THE RECORD, what happened later that night was the fault of only two people. The few friends who were on my side during this episode of my life tried to shift the blame to my former fiancé, because of the whole being-in-love-with-someone-else thing. I never blamed him, because I knew who the bad people were, and they were both in that hotel room.

Zack was not an issue when I agreed to have dinner with Manolo, and thoroughly enjoyed myself as we trashed the sheep we worked with and talked about our plans of dominating our respective offices. Zack was not an issue when I noticed that it was late, and instead of just going back up to the hotel room, asked Manolo to buy coffee and take it up with me. Not when Manolo placed the two takeout lattes on the little dining table and grabbed my left forearm with his right hand, hooked the curve of my neck with his left hand, or when my hands went up to cradle his jaw and lead his mouth to mine.

If Zack had been an issue at all, none of that would have happened, so I wasn't going to allow him to be blamed for anything.

Manolo and I were uncharacteristically wordless throughout the whole thing. I was afraid if I said something I would break the spell. We were sober and knew what we were doing, and I asked myself just how stupid this was. Maybe if I didn't talk I could pretend that we were in an alternate reality, one where Manolo didn't have a history of being such a jerk, and I didn't have a history of forgetting it. I would swear that he thought the same way, because he didn't say anything either.

Even without words, we were wonderfully coordinated, if I may say so myself. I decided I wanted to lick the underside of his chin and he turned his head aside to give me easy access. As soon as I slipped my feet out of my shoes he kicked them out of the way. My tailored top had a zipper that ran down one side, but before I could do anything about it he was already there, getting it out of the way, hands on my skin. *When did he figure that out?* If I closed my eyes and brought back selected memories, he still felt *good* to me. Better. He knew where to put his hands now, in unexpected places that made me tremble, like a particular bone in my back, or the curve of my hip.

Clothing scattered, piece by piece, as we made our way to the bed. He managed to stealthily remove a condom packet from his wallet before tossing said wallet in the general direction of the night table, which it missed, bouncing off the walls instead.

Many instances of sporadically making out and we

never got to this point. Still, it was like I knew his body—nothing about it surprised me. How his chest would feel against my palms. How his tongue would feel between my breasts. It was the same for him, I was sure of it. His breath didn't even hitch when I felt up and down those abs of his. I wrapped my hand around his erection, feeling it hard and smooth and thick and I *knew*. I wasn't going to be stopping this. Yes, worst timing in the world but when did we ever do that part right? We had our own time, picked up wherever and whatever we had left off.

It was obvious, at least to me, that he had done this before, and even when he discovered that I hadn't, he didn't say anything. No talking. I caught his eye and couldn't help it—I let my guard down and for the first time held him without contempt or irony. His next kiss felt like the first real one we'd shared.

THE DEED WAS DONE, so to speak, when Marjorie came into the room unexpectedly way past midnight. When it happened I thought I could still spin it. I could have claimed that Marjorie interrupted us "before anything could happen" and passed myself off as a repentant almost-sinner, but no, it was over.

I didn't even see her, but only she had access to the room too. She had probably seen me and Manolo on the bed, and left before saying or doing anything, but she didn't even need to. She broke the spell.

"Is this going to be a problem?" Manolo said, speaking a full sentence for the first time in hours.

I rubbed my eyes with my hands, sensing a headache coming on. "Yes, but I'll handle it."

I didn't wait to see him go. He started dressing but I couldn't bear to see him out, so I turned away and just closed my eyes. When I woke up the next morning, the lattes were untouched on the table. Manolo didn't show up at the conference that last day.

And that started the chain of events that ended with my wedding being called off. I could have blamed Marjorie, because if she didn't see that, then word of it would not have gotten to Zack. But ultimately, it didn't matter.

I knew that the cause of the drama was not that my indiscretion was discovered, but that it was committed at all. Obviously I was not over this guy, and I couldn't say for sure that this vicious cycle wouldn't pick up again in the future. If this was the reason why my relationship fell apart in such a humiliating fashion, then no one else was to blame but me and the other guy in the hotel room.

It wasn't that I couldn't tell Chesca. I couldn't tell *anybody*. But she, as always, thought it was about her.

EIGHTEEN

Now

THE BRIDE and her maid of honor endured icy silence in the car on the rest of the drive to BGC, and still as they walked into the condo unit rented for the day.

We stubbornly stuck to our schedule though. I still took her to the room because everyone thought that I was throwing the shower for her, and she went with me because it was still her party.

So the shower continued, except that we weren't speaking to each other. Chesca put a smile on her face and hugged and air-kissed her cousins and other guests, but made an effort not to look at me.

Isabel noticed, but wished she didn't. "What happened?"

Chesca was getting her toenails painted in one of the bedrooms and was out of earshot. I shrugged, not having the strength to even be angry. "Chesca."

"I can't leave the two of you alone."

"No you can't," I agreed. "But it's all beyond you, really."

She nibbled a triangle-shaped sandwich thoughtfully. "Kimmy, can't you...I don't know...be *nice*? Don't provoke her."

"What? I'm here. I'm present for every item on her wedding agenda."

"You're not the most cooperative person though."

"*She's* being all snappish, not me. This is a nice place, by the way." I changed the topic as soon as I could, to prevent Isabel from demonstrating further why I should be nice to Chesca. It was true, by the way. The apartment was nicely decorated, but a little too swanky for me.

"Wish you had gotten this instead?"

"Too big. And I'm sure I can't afford this building yet."

A weird look passed through her face all of a sudden. "Yeah but I wouldn't have shown you anything in this building anyway."

"What, you have no faith in me? I bet you I can afford this in a year. How much is it?"

"It's not that." She turned her back to me and went to the dining table to get a glass.

"Hey, cryptic. What are you talking about?"

She sighed. Isabel, you see, was always the level-headed one. While Chesca and I fought like kids, Isabel watched us from the sidelines and shook her head. Even if she often knew the smarter decision, she wasn't Chesca—she knew she didn't get to decide what was good for me or not.

"Manolo lives in this building," she admitted. "I helped him get the place last year."

"Really?" I tried so very hard to keep casual. "Interesting. Which floor?"

"Kimmy..."

"Sab, we're on the same side here."

"Going to his place alone is a bad idea."

"I know that. But what I eventually do or not do is not for you to decide and you know that, so you're going to tell me where he lives anyway."

Isabel pouted. "Twenty-seven eleven."

"Thank you."

"Please don't self-destruct. We just got you back." Her phone started ringing and she gave me an annoyed look as she picked it up. "Hello?"

Twenty-seven eleven. I repeated it so I wouldn't forget, and realized that he had a similar unit to the one we were in right now, just higher up.

"It's Tita Erica," Isabel said, handing her phone to me.

"Mom?"

"Kimmy!" My mom sounded not panicked or annoyed, but *inconvenienced.* "You really should get a phone now. Trying to find you is so stressful."

"You know where I am. You just had to call one person."

"You know what I mean. Your office called. They want you to come in right now."

"What? I can't. I don't start until Monday."

"Someone named Marjorie called me and said you have to come in today, right now, it's very urgent."

Ugh. Was Marjorie really determined to just ruin as many things for me as possible? "Ignore her," I told my mother. "I'm in the middle of a bridal shower!"

"Kimmy, she sounded serious. I know she's just going to keep calling me. And she found me because I'm listed as your emergency contact. I think she's quite desperate."

As expected, Chesca did not like this development, and hearing me say it broke the dam.

"I can't believe you." Chesca went from massage bliss to red-faced yelling in about three seconds. "I've had enough!

I do *everything* to involve you and you just keep doing this!"

"Doing what? It's a work emergency. I'm sorry but I really need to go."

"You keep *leaving*!" She pushed herself up from the bed and furiously tied her bathrobe around her. "I thought if I gave you the chance you'd at least try to be a friend again but you obviously don't want to be here. Fine! I give up!"

Any other person would have found this very awkward, what with the dozen people in the condo plus the spa therapists all being witness to this scene, but Chesca and I fought like this several times already. How else would we fight? We didn't know a discreet way to do it.

"They just need me to do something, I'm sure! I'll be back before you know it."

"Don't even," she said coldly. "And you know what? Don't even show up tomorrow. I don't want you at my wedding!"

Isabel dragged me away before we said more things that we'd regret.

"AND WE'RE GOOD?"

"Yes, bitch."

"I love you, Farrah. I mean it. Do you want to get married? I'll marry you. Just don't cancel on me."

"Glad you can joke about that now. But, Kimmy, all you have to do is not call me about this ever again. See you soon, babe."

I set down the phone. Marjorie was biting her finger (a stress thing, she didn't even realize she was doing it) as she looked at me.

"It's in," I said. "The revised feature will make it in the issue."

Marjorie slumped into her chair and her eyes were tearing up from relief. That was a strange reaction, I thought, because I on the other hand was exhilarated.

Five and half hours ago, when I casually walked into the office after being thrown out of Chesca's shower and wedding, Marjorie was in what I would call a shitload of trouble. It started with an executive lunch on Tuesday, when for the sake of building up her reputation with our Department VP she mentioned an upcoming major feature on a popular teen magazine, prominently displaying our new sunblock and the gorgeous male and female celebrity couple they picked to endorse it.

At the time that she bragged about this, she didn't know that there was a news item going around with a thinly veiled reference to the female celebrity having done very obvious cosmetic surgery while she was away on vacation. And because it was just that kind of week, on that same day (but later that night) the male celebrity got into a fistfight at a club known for fistfights, and the occasional drug bust.

One of our company's big bosses had a fit over the girl no longer looking like the expensive photograph they planned to launch the campaign with. Another boss had a son-in-law who was on the other side of the fistfight. Worse, it all landed on Marjorie's lap on the day after the magazine closed its issue and headed to printing.

She did her best, as far as I could tell. She found out if the two celebrities were going to be replaced (yes) and she found suitable substitutes. What she couldn't do herself was get the magazine to delay printing to make the switch.

Hence the emergency phone call to my mother.

I suspected this about Marjorie before, but now I knew

it to be true—she worked hard, but only delivered what the job required. She was probably one of those good students in college who studied hard, and played not at all.

The magazine in question was where Farrah, my friend the beauty editor, worked, and I spent the past few hours "working out" something with her and her publisher.

What mattered was that in the end, the replacement feature was going to make it, and Marjorie wasn't going to have to take back what she said to the VP, and the celebrity couple will probably spend the next weekend doing damage control on TV but it wouldn't be our immediate concern.

"You're welcome," I said.

She looked at me, like she had forgotten I was there. "Right. Yeah. Thanks, Kimmy."

"Relax. It's over."

"It's not over until I have that issue in my hands."

"Yeah, but we've done what we can."

"I guess. But thank you, Kimmy. Really. Couldn't have done it without you." Marjorie leaned back against her chair and just let it rock slowly.

I checked the clock on the wall of her office and noticed that in an hour and a half, Chesca's rehearsal dinner would start. If I were still invited to it I barely had enough time to go home and change and then make it back to the Intramuros restaurant where it was going to be. But then again I wasn't invited anymore. I could hang out a little longer.

"So why do you hate me, Marjorie?" I said, taking a seat on the other side of her table.

She hesitated. I waited a second to let it sink in.

"I don't hate you *now*," she said.

"But why did you, before?"

"Why does it matter? We're working together again and it's not relevant."

"Humor me," I said. "I've got nothing to do."

Marjorie pushed her chair back and shrugged. "You strike me as the type who always had it easy. You bat your eyelashes and everything just comes to you. And you're always so *smug* about it."

I laughed, remembering that I used the same word to describe someone else. "Fair enough. Maybe I just grew up overconfident."

"That too."

"But you don't hate me anymore?"

She raised an eyebrow at me. "It was easy to hate you when you had your eye on my boyfriend, but I've moved on. And he's moved on. It doesn't seem right to hate you for that anymore."

"Nothing happened with Zack while you were together, for your information."

"Nothing according to you."

"I'm not lying."

"I'm sure you're don't think you are. That's not the point. You probably believe you've done nothing wrong. You just act the way you act, and do what you do, and suddenly you have people eating out of your hand."

"Okay, I don't get that."

"Hmm, how do I translate," Marjorie shook her head and tried anyway. "This overconfident, overbearing *Kimmy* attitude you've got. It's off-putting. You think you didn't do anything to lure Zack away from me. But I've seen you flirt with him a zillion times, and to you it's just making conversation."

"I *was* just making conversation."

"See? That's it. You can't see things any other way but yours. And other people, like me, will interpret what you do our own way."

"Well," I replied, "if I may give you some feedback myself."

"Go ahead."

"This job? It's not just about getting this office. You have to invest in all these people who will help you. The assistants, accountants, security guards, people like Farrah and everyone else. They won't give you the time just because you flash that business card. That doesn't really mean anything."

"Are *you* giving me advice about being nice to other people?"

"It's not about being *nice*." Maybe I was saying it wrong. I recalled how I learned this lesson, from that summer watching Manolo work, and tried again. "You have to know who you need to be on your side to succeed, and then be their best friend."

"So you never thought you needed me? You never made me into your best friend here."

I sighed. Marjorie didn't get it, obviously, but it was her loss. "We're peers. Or we were. I was absolutely willing to work with you until you decided that I was competition and treated me like it. So I competed with you. But now you're my boss, and I know that I need you, and you can quit thinking I'm going to sabotage your career or something."

Another thing that surprised people: I didn't mind losing, if this could be considered losing. It wasn't, really. I just recognized when life gave me a bad deal and adjusted accordingly. Like it or not, this girl who hated me was now my boss. I could spend my energy fighting it, but the better way was to swallow my pride and just work with her.

So a truce between us was called, and I didn't have to see her again until Monday.

NINETEEN

The surprise visit to unit twenty-seven eleven was not such a surprise, thanks to the remarkably efficient building security.

"Can't I just go up? I know where it is," I told the lobby receptionist.

"Sorry, ma'am, we have to confirm with Mr. Mella first." He reached for the phone on his desk and called. "Sir? You have a guest here at the lobby. She's asking to go up to your floor."

Shit.

The guard looked at me. "Your name is?"

"Kimberly Domingo."

"Kimberly Domingo, sir," he said onto the phone. And then to me: "Ms. Domingo, Mr. Mella says that he's on his way out now, and you should just wait for him here."

"No," I told the guard. "Tell him to wait for me upstairs."

Manolo probably heard what I'd said, because the guard didn't have to repeat it. He just nodded and waved me through to the elevators.

"You're not dressed," he said, pointing out that I wasn't

in the "dinner semi-formal" required by Chesca for her rehearsal dinner. He, on the other hand, looked perfect.

I set down my bag, crossed the room, and kissed him. It was a light kiss, not like the usual dance where limbs and lips grabbed at each other. Instead, I gently reached for his face and brushed against his mouth, almost timidly.

If Manolo had been surprised, he recovered very quickly. He took me into his arms, and I let him do that, but I kept my senses intact. I was remembering the feel of his lips, the way he smelled right then, obviously after a shower, and the feel of his hands on my neck.

One thing I was sure of—he didn't notice anything different about me. He kissed the same way. He had the habit of letting me set the pace for a few moments, and then taking over, but I didn't go with it this time and kept pulling him back to the shallow end.

We wound up on his couch, and I sat there for what must have been fifteen minutes, not talking. It felt so good to just shut up—not fight, not complain, not spend time being skeptical of everything. He knew we were running late but everything was of end-of-the-world urgency to Chesca anyway, and let me be.

I wanted to say stuff, but wasn't sure how. As I wondered how I would start, he absently ran his finger down the length of the couch until it touched my elbow. It didn't go any further than that.

"What's wrong?" he said, finally.

"I've been kicked out of Chesca's wedding. I'm not going to the dinner tonight."

"You two fight all the time. It doesn't mean anything."

I shrugged. "This time I'm going to make it mean something. It's a toxic friendship. If she doesn't want me there I won't force myself."

"She *does* want you there."

"Yeah, it hasn't felt that way in a long time."

Manolo shook his head. "I don't understand the two of you. You're like kids."

"It's not like the both of you get along so well."

"I don't make fighting with her a sport. We just disagree on things."

"Well, I've decided that since I'm back, I can only make this work by getting out of this circle of people."

"What does that mean?"

"I'm moving out of my mom's house. I was going to drop Country Club brunches, but Chesca cutting me out of her wedding just made that easier."

"What did Tita Erica say about you moving out?"

Not the thing I was expecting him to react to. "Nothing. Typical Mom."

"I don't think moving out is the best idea for you now."

"What are you talking about? It's my decision."

"How can you afford it?"

"I'm cutting back on other things."

The emotion started to creep into his voice, and I was taken aback by it. "Don't you think that's a bit selfish?"

"She understands. She's done this before. She can't tell me *not* to do it."

"Maybe she can't *tell* you but you should think twice about it anyway."

"Manolo, you know what? Let my mother tell me what she does and doesn't want."

The smooth edges that always characterized Manolo for me were suddenly not so smooth. He was frustrated, and it made him seem like he was losing his cool. "You think she's told you everything? You've been back only a few days. You're proud that you avoided everyone, so you have no idea how we all are. Any decision you make right now about any of us just means you're not bothering to find out."

"You called me selfish."

"What would *you* call it?"

"Just because I finally found a way to make sure that I don't screw up my life this time? Think about it, Manolo—I'm not asking anybody to change for me. I'm actually doing all of you a favor by packing up and disappearing again. As much as I can while living here too, at least. Is that selfish?"

"All of us?" He caught that and threw it back at me. "What kind of favor are you doing me?"

Ah crap. I should have practiced this.

Manolo and I had never talked about "us." It used to be that way because he was a cool older guy who didn't want to, and then later I welcomed it because it was easier. But twelve years and all the drama later, not talking no longer felt right.

"I can't handle it anymore," I told him. "I've reached the limit of what I can take. I love you, but can't bear it when you come back like we have something, and then leave like there was nothing all along. I think it's just better if I stay out of your way."

"How are you going to manage that? This place can be a small town."

"It can be done. You know how. There were times when I didn't see you for years, and you showed up again only to mess me up."

It wasn't until his hand retreated when I realized that it had still been there, finger idly touching my elbow, this whole time. The separation felt sudden, even though when it was there I had forgotten it.

"Maybe you haven't changed," he said quietly, standing up. "I'm late for the rehearsal dinner."

"You don't have to drive me home," I said.

"I wasn't planning to." His voice was cold, and I felt that I was being kicked out. Before he closed the door behind me, he said, "Kimberly, I should tell you before you go through with this and avoid me completely—grow up. And talk to your mother."

TWENTY

Was it possible? Did I miss out on something?

The people in my life, they spoke their minds. We were critical of people who were too secretive. We laughed at those who weren't confident. Because of them I became this type of person, abrasive and all, but I rarely ever lied. I thought they would be the same toward me.

So what changed? *I* went through the very public humiliation. *I* spent the year away and discovered the same thing my mother did many years ago—that leaving was the best therapy. I delighted in the existence without drama, achieved only by taking myself away from them. Wouldn't my departure spare them all and result in everyone being at peace? They got to keep everything—their routines, traditions, a Country Club with the best of everything, and each other. I was willing to start from scratch with just the basics. How come *I* was the selfish one?

For the first time in what to me was a long time, I walked into my mother's bedroom. It was the master's bedroom, back then, designed especially for her. She liked big windows, even though it only gave her a spectacular view of the street and our neighbor's house. Her side of the bed was closest to the huge walk-in closet, where Chesca and I used to spend hours just playing with clothes and shoes.

I flipped the light on, and it was clean. Too clean.

Clean because it was nearly cleared out of furniture.

The bed was different. It used to be a king-sized mattress on heavy narra, with intricate carving on the headboard. As a kid I hated resting my back against it. Now it was a plain bed, indistinguishable from one in a guest bedroom.

The walk-in closet was almost entirely empty. The shelves and wardrobe nearest to the door still had recognizable clothes and shoes, but I suspected that it was only what was actually in use. The rest, they were gone.

At least the bed was more comfortable now. I made myself comfortable in the middle, back against the headboard, and waited for my mother to arrive.

AT FIRST, she didn't want to talk about it, but I wouldn't leave her bed.

"How bad is it?" I asked again.

"It's not bad," she insisted. "I just had a difficult year. That's all."

"That's *all*? Mom, last year this room was full of your stuff."

"There's still too much stuff."

"Where did it all go?"

"Kimmy, I'm tired. We had a long day. Let's just talk about this another time."

No, I wasn't going to let this go. Not after seeing what my mom had given up. "How bad is it?"

"I told you, it's not bad."

"You sold my car. You let go of Yaya. More than half your closet is *gone*. What's going on?" As I talked, and she didn't, I was being pushed toward some really bad thoughts. "Are you sick?"

"No I'm not."

"Is Lola? Lolo? Liz? Is Liz okay?"

"They're all fine. Your sister is fine."

"Well it can't all be *fine* and all of this is happening. What's wrong? What's different now?"

"Go to bed, Kimmy."

"I'm not leaving until you tell me."

"*Just go to bed.*" Mom tried to make that sound firm and snappish. Didn't work. I just returned the look, and I was reminded then of how much we looked alike. Maybe of how much we *were* alike.

"It's been a difficult year and you weren't here," Mom said.

"What did you need me for?" I asked.

Her shoes came off, but she didn't sit down. "Your dad has stopped helping us out."

"What? Why?"

"His new girlfriend thinks that he shouldn't be doing that anymore." There was bitterness in that sentence, a hint of what problems were in their past. Most of that she shielded me from.

"So that's why you've sold my car, and everything else?"

"Selling the car and everything else made it better. It's over, problem was solved. Asking about it now doesn't help me."

"You didn't call me to tell me this?"

Mom laughed, with sarcasm. "I tried. You of course preferred not to be contacted."

I didn't want to take anyone's phone calls because I thought that their bubble was impenetrable by these things. Nothing could ever really go wrong with the Country Club set; they would take care of themselves.

"How long have you had trouble with money?"

"It started maybe three months after you left," Mom said. "But selling your car, my jewelry and other stuff helped with what I needed last year. This year is another story, especially if your dad is serious about cutting me off."

"I'll talk to Dad."

"Don't do that."

"This is wrong."

"Don't talk to your dad, Kimmy. My life has been expensive to maintain. This isn't his problem anymore."

It was an expensive lifestyle; the upkeep on the house alone baffled me. Electricity charges never seemed to go down. It cost money to serve a full spread every single meal. One household having two cars was common for us, but everyone else in this country got by with less than that. And the Country Club, with its buffet meals, pools, and tennis courts—felt like home, but infinitely pricier.

While I was away, and this was happening, she never asked me to come back. She could have done that. Even if I had refused phone calls, she was the type who would have found me and yelled at me from overseas, if she wanted to. Instead she let me be, and solved her problems on her own.

I only had two people I intended to keep in my life, and I already let one of them down. Something kicked at my chest, something familiar now—shame. Not the kind that comes with everyone at work overhearing your sin, but the private one. The audience and victim was just one person, and she would likely never tell anybody.

I was wrong, this felt *so* much worse.

"I'm sorry," I said, my voice again like a child. I was trying not to cry; I had no right to. "I'm sorry. Maybe I shouldn't move out."

"Maybe you need to, just for a bit. However long your lease is. I never intended to keep you *in this house* forever... I just wanted you to be in touch."

"I'm sorry."

She sighed. "Last year is over. What's done is done."

"Manolo was helping you out all year, wasn't he?" I wondered if she would ever reveal how much. Throughout this conversation her pride was very much intact.

"His mom really did prove she's my best friend. I owe a lot to their family."

"I'll help out more."

"I'll believe that when I see it."

I wanted to hug her, but when I started to get up to do that, she nonchalantly headed to her dresser, like we were just having a normal conversation. She pulled out a white letter envelope.

"Manolo asked me to mail this to you, months ago. He said he had emailed you and you wouldn't reply, but I didn't know if by the time I sent this you'd still be at your tita's. So I just kept it."

I took the envelope, curious. It wasn't sealed. "Did you read it?"

Mom looked at me and did a half-roll of her eyes. "Of course I did."

KIMBERLY,

EVEN IF I said that I loved you, I know that you'd say that I couldn't possibly because I've put you through too much shit. And I would tell you that I was a dumb kid who thought he knew everything. I enjoy our banter. I don't have the same relationship with anyone else.

Anyone else would have been happy with that, but I kept avoiding it. Our families don't seem to understand how we can both get. If they did they wouldn't be pushing us together like they do.

And you know we would fight. Nothing that would make me hate you. Nothing you've ever told me has made me hate you. But you know how much our moms meddle. They'd be as much a part of our relationship and I didn't want that.

If we were in a relationship.

Kimmy, talk to me. Email at least. I'm sure if you saw how much I've lost focus and sleep because of you, you'd come out of hiding just to laugh at me.

Right now I'd take it. I don't care if our families get hurt. They'll deal. Talk to me.

HE DIDN'T SIGN IT, except I knew his handwriting from when we worked together and I watched him take notes.

I finally checked my email.

TWENTY-ONE

The first email from him was the week after my flight from Manila to LA.

Kimmy,

Do you have a number I can call?

The next one was three weeks later.

I get it. You're not contacting anyone. But I want to talk to you. You know where to call me. It doesn't matter what time it is. Was it something I did?

A week later:

So still not talking to me.

You're not talking to anyone either, I've checked, so I don't know if this retreat of yours is because of me.

But in case it's about me, thanks for giving me hell by not telling me.

You have to call me. If this is shocking to you and the reason why you left is not at all about us, then have a laugh at my expense and don't mention this again.

The next day:

I rambled yesterday. I forgot something. I love you. At this point I feel like I'm talking to my laptop.

The last one was a few months ago, and it looked like it was dated after the letter he had handed to my mom:

I'm moving into a new place. I won't be at the country club as much. They talk about you all the time there, trying to figure out where you are and what you're doing, and I can't listen to it anymore. If you're coming back, when you come back, talk to me.

There were one thousand three hundred and eight unread emails waiting for me, and believe it or not there were a few more that took me by surprise.

I was reading Manolo's emails—and thinking about them—until three in the morning.

At seven-thirty Mom knocked on my door and asked if I really wasn't going to the wedding. I yelled that it wasn't my choice. Then she left for her hair appointment, and since I couldn't go back to sleep, I looked at my email again.

A recent one, from Isabel, was strange. The subject line was "Pics from Chesca's Despedida de Soltera," and I clicked on it without even thinking.

About a dozen web-resolution photos were attached. I thought that this was old school of her, people rarely attached their photos in email now, but then I caught something strange.

Chesca was wearing a different dress in the photos.

I went through the attachments and noticed that *everyone* was wearing different clothing. Tita Chat, my mom, Isabel, although the party was obviously still in the same place. The other thing? *I* wasn't in any of the photos.

Another email from Isabel: "Dinner with Chavez family." Same thing. Everyone was wearing something else, and there were a few people in the photos that I didn't see at the dinner. And then a group photo with more detail revealed that it wasn't even the same restaurant.

Shit, Chesca. What have you been doing?

The third email from her ("Shower pics!"), like the others, showed pictures of an entirely different bridal shower, one that didn't have me in it.

I checked the dates for the emails, all of them were from last week.

TWENTY-TWO

Friday

Chesca and Andrew's Wedding

MY WEDDING WAS SUPPOSED to have been held at a glass pavilion a half-hour drive from home. My dad had decided that he would fly to Manila to give me away. My sister rearranged a US trip to make it. A pastor who had been counseling my mother for many years had agreed to officiate. I was supposed to be married in a small outdoor ceremony with family and a few friends only, as the sun was setting, and then proceed to have dinner with three hundred guests at the reception.

Chesca's was set for a late morning ceremony at the place where her parents were married, a church in Manila. A lunch reception would follow at a hotel near Manila Bay. It was a little unconventional to have a wedding on a regular Friday at lunch, because most of the guests would normally be at work or school, but Chesca wanted it that way. She wanted people to commit to be there because they loved her, and not because it was a convenient time.

Well sure it wasn't convenient. I went against my principles and offered double the fare to a taxi driver just so he'd take me all the way to the church.

Thankfully, once I realized what I had to, I had all I needed at home. The altered maid-of-honor dress was in a dry cleaning bag in the living room. The shoes Chesca wanted me to wear were in a box on top of the dining table. As soon as I got out of the shower, the next crucial minutes were spent styling my hair, and then I just threw pressed powder, blush, and lipstick into a little bag. I applied makeup in the taxi and hassled the driver about getting to Manila in less than an hour.

He failed me. It was fifteen minutes after the ceremony was supposed to start when we got even remotely in the vicinity. As we turned the corner I was fighting with him about decisions he made on the road, but still handed him the promised fare as I stepped out of the cab and ran toward the church.

The ground was gravel, and I nearly tripped over myself a few times. When I got close enough to the entrance of the church I was stopped by a familiar person.

"Kimmy?" Isabel had grabbed me by the wrist. She was dressed in her lovely ivy green bridesmaid dress and was out of breath. She'd been running after me just as I got out of the cab. "You made it!"

"Where's Chesca?"

"Still in the bridal car. But you shouldn't stress her out, wedding's about to start—"

The white Volvo with a flower arrangement on its nose was parked right in front of the church. Thank God for old-school weddings that never started on time. I was pretty sure I had at least fifteen more minutes when I joined the surprised bride inside the car.

"What are you doing here?"

"Oh shut up, Chesca." I said, making sure my dress was completely inside the car before slamming the door shut. "I saw the pics from your other shower. And you were going to tell me about it when?"

"Fuck. I'm still mad at you. Get out of my bridal car!" Her hands formed little fists that punched ineffectively into my dress.

Oh, Chesca and I fought a lot, but when did it last involve hands and hair? Must have been when we were kids. I spent most of my energy grabbing her wrists and making sure she didn't mess up her own hair and makeup. The winning move was when I pulled a wrist down and pinned it to the seat. She stopped to breathe, and I managed to look her in the eye.

"If you're that mad at me, why did you do all of this for me?"

Chesca looked stunning, by the way. She had a way of looking unaffected by everything while it was very obvious on my face that I lacked sleep and my makeup had been applied in transit.

What I had realized, after seeing the third set of photos from Isabel, was that Chesca already had her wedding parties last week. A despedida de soltera at her house, a dinner with Andrew's family, and a bridal shower, all last week—without me.

Which meant that all the events I had been to this week had been staged *for me*. Because I had missed them. Because I didn't take her calls, didn't go back home when she wanted me to. So she threw all the parties again, just for me.

It was love, Chesca style. Sneaky, and more complicated than it needed to be. I couldn't help but feel like the champion of all the selfish.

She pulled her hand out with a huff. "It wasn't just me. It was Manolo's idea too."

"So you're best friends now? When did that happen?"

"Since he came to me and said that I should be nicer to you because you and your mom are going through something. I told him that was stupid—if Tita Erica or my Best Friend Since Birth Kimmy needed me, they'd ask for help. And they haven't asked me for help."

Not if we didn't know what we needed, apparently.

"Why did you still do it?" I asked. "Even if I didn't ask for anything. Even if I was selfish for not coming home when you wanted me to."

She was incensed at that. "*Why*? Are you kidding me? I'm actually disappointed you didn't figure it out earlier. I mean, who holds all their wedding parties three days before their wedding? That's just opening the door and letting a world of stress inside! Of course I planned all of my parties way in advance. But you insisted on not coming home last week."

"So you and Manolo just put everyone up to it?"

It was easy, for Chesca at least. Tita Chat always threw parties at home anyway. Andrew's family needed a little convincing, but they came around eventually. She told everyone not to mention it, but she hadn't anticipated that Isabel our "good stepsister" would do something else entirely. And Manolo, apparently, paid for everything related to the repeat events.

I had been so self-absorbed about my coming home, keeping my head held high after my shameful departure. It didn't even occur to me that *I* wasn't on everyone's mind anymore. It was Chesca's time.

I owed it to her to be honest, after all of this. "Chesca, when I came back I was planning to just sit through this wedding and then cut you off."

"Cut me off? What the hell?"

"I'm moving out of my mom's house. I won't be visiting the Country Club every week anymore."

"What, and that includes dumping me from your schedule?"

"I don't think I ever talked about why I left. I was really messed up, and I blamed two people for it."

I told her, for the first time, about the night at the hotel with Manolo, and it put her knowledge of the events that followed in a whole new light. Minutes later she lifted a finger to her eye, and I saw that she was trying to catch a tear that was about to fall. She didn't; it rolled a wet streak down her cheek.

"You blame me for that?" she said. "You never told me what had happened. I wouldn't have forced you to stay with Zack if I knew."

"No, that's not what you would have said."

"What are you talking about?"

The Worst Maid of Honor Ever didn't have a tissue and instead reached forward and gently brushed a tear from the bride's face with the back of her hand. "You would have said that I should be happy that I scratched that itch, keep it a secret, and go ahead and marry Zack anyway."

Chesca blinked, and two more tears fell, and she started laughing. "Oh my God. Yes I would have said that."

"See? You're horrible."

"I'm realistic. I've been trying to save you from him. But

of course I've been a failure at it. You are as in love with him as you were when we were kids."

Maybe that was part of the problem with the three of us. Chesca, Manolo and I—we always treated each other the exact same way we did when we were young and stupid. I may not have agreed with her methods, or her purposes, but she was always looking for out for me, and at the very least deserved better.

And if I wanted her to understand me and leave me alone, I should have just said so, instead of acting out and taking extreme steps.

"I missed you," she said, and I felt her sincerity. "I was planning my wedding without you. I always thought we would plan this together."

"I'm here now."

"Are you sane again?"

"Maybe. But thank you for not giving up on me."

"Oh please. I haven't forgiven you yet."

The strange thing was? I felt bad, but didn't regret much. I knew she did too. Chesca felt entirely justified about all her actions, and so did I. The point wasn't to change anyone's mind, but to accept each other as the controlling, flawed people that we were.

"What can I do?" I said. "I've been the worst maid of honor. I have to make it up to you somehow."

Chesca opened the door on her side and yelled for her stylist to come over. Then, to me: "Let's see if you can get through this wedding without ruining it for me. Then we can talk about forgiveness."

TWENTY-THREE

The wedding of Francesca Lara Martin to John Andrew Chavez was, I grudgingly admitted to myself, hard to top.

I wasn't into large, old churches, but the history, the flowers, the formal wear—it gave the ceremony that extra bit of drama. Andrew read his own vows, and Chesca cried over hers, but she looked gorgeous, and I was genuinely happy for her.

When I wasn't happy for her I was stealing glances over to the other side of the altar, where the best man stood in his tailored barong.

He didn't speak to me, and barely even looked at me, as far as I could tell. Surely he was surprised when he saw me walk down the aisle. When the ceremony ended and the photos at the church were taken, he was nowhere near me, and I didn't get the chance to say hello.

When everyone filed into their vehicles for the trip to the reception, he was one of the first to leave, and I took a ride there with my mother instead.

At the reception itself, in the ballroom of a hotel by the bay, we were seated on opposite ends of the same table.

If last night—from the visit to his place to reading his emails—hadn't happened, the cold shoulder of today wouldn't have been a big deal. I would have dismissed it as one of those many times when he didn't bother to be nice to me. But now the silence was in response to my request, and I knew that I could end the silence if I asked.

I didn't know how to, though. Not after I made such a big deal about staying away.

Lunch was served. The menu was Spanish themed, and I took little bites of paella and cocido just so I wouldn't collapse, but I wasn't very hungry. A professional host talked us through the program. She showed a video specially prepared for the wedding reception, featuring photos of Chesca and Andrew through the years. They looked like they were grabbed from her scrapbook collection, and I sadly acknowledged that there were some photos there that I had never seen before. Probably taken during my year away.

Chesca's parents spoke. They told us how much they loved their daughter, how proud they were of her, and how Andrew should never leave his dirty clothes on the floor if he knew what was good for him. Andrew's parents talked about welcoming Chesca to their family, and how they appreciated that she brought the best out of their son.

The host offered the microphone to the best man and the maid of honor, but Chesca shook her head vehemently.

"No," she said, deadpan. "Please don't. This is my night, and I won't be upstaged by my dramatic entourage."

So I spent most of the reception without speaking, and let my best friend have the best night of her life.

THREE HOURS of eating and gossiping later, and people started to leave. I felt obligated to stay behind, though, to compensate for flaking out on Chesca one too many times. I was polite and on my best behavior with all of the relatives, and even spent some time hopping tables to talk to the guests.

When the reception was winding down, I took a nice, long walk around the hotel. I spent time at the gift shop, browsed the menu at the café, took my time at the powder room, eased into small talk with the concierge. Five hours, no drama. It was refreshing. I could get used to this.

Isabel caught up with me when I walked out onto the garden by the pool, and for the first time that day we talked about me. I had tried to not make the day about me. "So what happened, Kimmy?"

"I read my email. Saw the stuff you sent."

She sighed. "Good. Finally."

"You sent me the pictures but you didn't tell me to do anything. What were you expecting to happen?"

Isabel shrugged. "I don't know. Maybe if you saw it last week you'd be so angry that you weren't part of it that you'd come home. Except when you got here you really didn't have any idea."

"Or I could have seen it last week and decided not to come home at all."

"I'm glad you and Chesca made up."

"Why didn't you just tell me?"

"Are you kidding me? I wanted to. I told her that if the two of you have problems you should just talk."

"She's so difficult."

"You're both difficult." Isabel was exasperated, but in that loving way of hers. "But you know why I don't just refuse to see either of you ever again? Because you're family.

And you've both grown up and changed. You're both quite amazing actually, if you bothered to see it."

"I came today because I realized that if I can't forgive her and love her as she is, then I can't expect anyone to do the same for me."

Being there also made me see that though she was sneaky and manipulative and annoying, Chesca was loved by so many people. Genuinely. It was obvious in the way Andrew looked at her, the way her parents talked about her, and in the smiles of all the guests.

How could I hate someone so loved by the people who mattered? Maybe I was the defective one. I didn't have the close-knit family, or the supportive cousins, or the adoring boyfriend. I had friendships, but not love in my life. Not like this.

That was something I didn't even tell Chesca, but Isabel was my conscience. It felt like something I could tell my conscience. "Isabel, I don't want to prove people right. I don't want people to think I deserve punishment."

Her hand had been on my arm, but then it pulled me into a hug. "Kimmy, do you really think people think that?"

"Yes," I sniffled into her hair. "Yes they do."

"I can't believe this. You have your mom, and me, and Chesca. We'll do anything for you, you know that."

That was nice of her to say, but it didn't change the fact that I had a way of alienating people who would have cared about me. That was my fault, not anyone else's.

I remembered someone who *had* done a lot for me, and I had yet to thank.

I grabbed a bottle of champagne, and tapped the shoulder of the best man.

"Would you please step outside with me for a second?" I asked.

THIS ALMOST LOOKED like a way to undo the past—here we were, back in a wedding, by the pool, with a bottle of champagne. It was tempting to see this as a magical moment, a chance to go back and "do it right this time."

But, I learned that I can't take back anything. I've said and done hurtful things and it didn't matter that I didn't mean them; only children are not held accountable for the stupid things they say and do. I *was* hurtful, and selfish, and maybe I *was* punished.

"I talked to my mom," I said.

"Good." It was a grunt, both distant and resentful.

It wasn't just me and Chesca who had grown up. He *was* different now. Not that he suddenly changed, but if I saw him as he was *now*, I would see him as a successful, witty, driven young man, and not the eighteen-year-old who broke my heart. And maybe he had started seeing me as an accomplished young woman, and not the petty fifteen-year-old who kept picking a fight.

"I've been in love with you since I was in high school," I said, just letting it out. "And it messed me up. But I'm not going to blame other people for my shit anymore. If I regret anything, it's that I didn't tell you all of this right after. That I didn't call off the wedding myself. And while I was away I stayed up most nights without sleeping, kept thinking of what I should have done, like I wish that I hadn't been scared by Marjorie showing up, or that I should have said something to make you stay. Or that I should have called you the next day and said this. But I couldn't, because I hate how pathetic it all sounds."

It was word vomit. At some point I couldn't stop *telling the truth*.

"What else did your mom tell you?" he asked.

"She gave me your letter."

Something flickered in his face, and he grabbed onto the nearest lounge chair and sat on it. "It was never mailed."

"It's not her fault. She wasn't sure where to send it."

"She read it, didn't she?"

"You know my mother."

He shook his head. "She probably told my mom. And that's why they haven't bugged me about you so much recently."

"They never knew how you felt about it."

So we liked to speak our minds, but not our hearts. Too bad, because sometimes people needed to hear that. A whole mess of things could have been avoided if we just knew how to say the right thing.

"My mom is beyond grateful for what you've done for her," I told him, sincerely. "If she hasn't said it exactly that way, you should know that that's how she feels."

"How do you feel?"

"I just told you."

"That was all the past. How do you feel now?"

I took a deep breath. "I want to apologize for how I've treated you, especially the past few days. I owe it to you to get to know you again, as you are now."

That was as mature as he had ever heard me, and it made him laugh. "That sounds responsible of you."

"I'm trying. I've been selfish all this time. This caring about people takes getting used to."

"I still love you."

"Don't be so sure. It's been a while since you wrote that."

"I think we should try to make this work, and if it doesn't then we can end this once and for all. Disappearing won't work. Trust me, I've tried to leave many times, but I keep coming back."

My instinct was to attack, not believe him, say something to protect myself from this thing that sounded nice right now but was statistically proven to cause me pain in the future. That was our history.

"Are you still the kind of guy who hits on girls at conferences?" I had to know.

"I'm not the kind of guy who hits on girls at conferences."

"I heard that you were."

"I only did that once. I think you'll remember." He straightened up and inched toward me. "You ready to do this?"

Could I really count on things being different this time?

No, but *I* was going to be different. If changing one thing about this averts the disaster, then I hope that this would be that thing.

What mattered was that everyone I hated, but loved, was still around. *Maybe I should end my pity party and make it work while they still think I'm worth the trouble.*

This time it was my hand on his neck, taking my kiss.

"Yes," I said, just in case it wasn't clear what my answer was.

EPILOGUE

Years later

"I THINK WE SHOULD GET MARRIED."

Wow. What? It wasn't Roleplay Friday. Sometimes, when it was my turn to tell him what to do, I made him act against type. Say things he'd never say. My entire brain blinked, or it felt like it, when he said this. It seemed like a Not Manolo thing to say.

It wasn't Roleplay Friday, but it *was* his birthday. Sometimes he made special requests on his birthday, and they'd always been a little dirty. *Wear this. Say this. Let's try it like this.*

This was by far the dirtiest birthday request yet.

I did not respond.

"I'm waiting," he said.

"You're not serious." This was unsettling, for a bunch of reasons. My history with weddings, for one. Number two, it seemed like it was out of character for him. And number three, I was *in my underwear*. Not even sexy naughty ones because he showed up back in his own condo early for the birthday dinner we were supposed to go to, and caught me still eating chips on his couch. He sprung the question on me as he leaned against the doorway to his bedroom, while I was pulling my dress for the night from his closet. This moment would be immortalized in my memory, and I was wearing a functional strapless bra and black bikini cut panties. Not out of the ordinary for me to be walking around his place wearing just those, but *the moment.*

He was in a blazer, a crisp shirt, and a great tie. All black, which was considerate of him. He knew how I liked him.

Manolo couldn't have waited one minute to start talking?

"Think about it," he said, still talking.

I slipped the dress on, which took like ten seconds, and he could have waited ten damn seconds. "I considered the concept, before. Didn't work out. Why are *you* thinking about it?"

He looked unruffled. "You want a list of reasons?"

"It would be nice to know what you've been thinking about, birthday boy." I really wasn't expecting this. And honestly, I told myself to be ready for whatever kinky thing he wanted today. I was excited and worked up for...well, not this. "I mean, I understand why you think it would be practical..."

"Practical."

My pointy shiny slingback heels were waiting beside the closet door and those were on me in two damn seconds. "Yes. Because I'm spending half the time at your place now? Because I keep my wine and cheese here, which makes sense because your kitchen is nicer?"

"That's not a bad thing, as far as I'm concerned."

"Because...because you're getting older? Way past thirty now, not that you look ancient. But your dad and uncles are silver foxes, so there's that to look forward to—well for me at least. Worried you'll be old and alone, darling?"

"Are you done trying to figure me out?"

"Did I?"

"You forgot that I love you."

It was always a tiny shock to the system, to hear him say it. To know he meant it. To understand the truth of it, finally. This was love, the way we both liked to do love. No one else would get it.

"You do," I said, not hiding it under a layer of snark this time. "But I'm sure you considered the risk factors. My parents are separated. I didn't get to have a wedding. I almost ruined my best friend's wedding. This is not my favorite topic."

"I was there." Of course he was. "I accept all of that. Kimmy, you can do this however you want."

"What are you talking about? Marriage is—everyone knows what that means. They do it differently now?"

He sighed, but not out of impatience. Just his usual Kimmy's-being-Kimmy sigh. "I mean I want this, always. You. Me. Officially, so all the things we build together are ours. So we get to enjoy what's ours. And we can do it any way you want it. If you don't want a big wedding, we won't do that. If you don't want anyone to know, we won't tell anyone. If you don't want to get married, well..."

"You'll take it?" I asked. "You'll accept it, even if I say no?"

"Yes."

"No way."

"It's a suggestion. You know it makes sense. But it's just...a suggestion."

It made sense for sure to someone with a family like the Mellas. Property, inheritance...they considered these things, and pieces of paper mattered. Did it matter to me?

"Whatever your answer," he said, "it doesn't change how I feel about you. What you are to me."

"No way."

"Try me."

"It *has* been a while. This you and me situation."

"You seem to be enjoying yourself."

I am. We are.

I hooked my arm around his and then my lips were on his mouth. Fine. Maybe it didn't matter where we were, or what I was wearing.

"Happy birthday," I told Manolo. "I love you."

"You'll marry me?"

I didn't think I'd ever marry anyone, after that first mistake. I didn't think I'd ever want to, again.

"I'll let you know," I said. "I need to think about it."

He kissed me. It was a good kiss, an interesting proposition. It made me jittery still, to think that I deserved this.

I could start believing.

The End

AUTHOR'S NOTE

Thank you for reading Kimmy's story.

Kimmy Domingo's first appearance was in My Imaginary Ex, my first book. Love Your Frenemies was released two years later, and I treasure the reactions I got. (And am still getting.) This book connects me to interesting people; I can only guess why.

This edition has a new epilogue. It's a bridge, really. To see a little more into Kimmy and Manolo's future, you can read *Iris After the Incident* (Chic Manila #8). The new cover was designed by Tania Arpa, featuring AJ Olpindo and Coralin Resurreccion. Thank you, Katt and Dawn, for casting my Manolo and Kimmy. Thank you, Pach and Alex, for making it happen in the studio.

- Mina

CHIC MANILA SERIES BY MINA V. ESGUERRA

Contemporary romances set in the Philippines. Can be read as standalones.

My Imaginary Ex (#1), Jasmine and Zack
Fairy Tale Fail (#2), Ellie and Lucas
No Strings Attached (#3), Carla and Dante
Love Your Frenemies (#4), Kimmy and Manolo
That Kind of Guy (#5), Julie and Anton
Welcome to Envy Park (#6), Moira and Ethan
What You Wanted (#7), Andrea and Damon
Iris After the Incident (#8), Iris and Gio
Better At Weddings Than You (#9), Daphne and Aaron

ABOUT THE AUTHOR

Mina V. Esguerra writes contemporary romance, young adult, and new adult novellas. Visit her website minavesguerra.com for more about her books, talks, and events.

When not writing romance, she is president of communications firm Bronze Age Media, development communication consultant, and indie publisher. She created the workshop series "Author at Once" for writers and publishers, and #romanceclass for aspiring romance writers. Her young adult/fantasy trilogy Interim Goddess of Love is a college love story featuring gods from Philippine mythology. Her contemporary romance novellas won the Filipino Readers' Choice awards for Chick Lit in 2012 (Fairy Tale Fail) and 2013 (That Kind of Guy).

She has a bachelor's degree in Communication and a master's degree in Development Communication.

Addison Hill series: Falling Hard | Fallen Again | Learning to Fall

Breathe Rockstar Romance series: Playing Autumn | Tempting Victoria | Kissing Day (short story)

Chic Manila series: My Imaginary Ex | Fairy Tale Fail | No Strings Attached | Love Your Frenemies | That Kind of Guy | Welcome to Envy Park | Wedding Night Stand (short story) | What You Wanted | Iris After the Incident | Better At Weddings Than You

Scambitious series: Young and Scambitious | Properly Scandalous | Shiny and Shameless | Greedy and Gullible

Interim Goddess of Love series: Interim Goddess of Love | Queen of the Clueless | Icon of the Indecisive | Gifted Little Creatures (short story) | Freshman Girl and Junior Guy (short story)

The Future Chosen

Anthology contributions: Say That Things Change (New Adult Quick Reads 1) | Kids These Days: Stories from Luna East Arts Academy Volume 1 | Sola Musica: Love Notes from a Festival | Make My Wish Come True | Summer Feels

Contact Mina

minavesguerra.com
minavesguerra@gmail.com

BOOKS BY FILIPINO AUTHORS
#ROMANCECLASS

Visit romanceclassbooks.com to read more
romance/contemporary/YA by Filipino authors.

Made in the USA
Middletown, DE
24 August 2022

72165883R00083